THE ATTIC MURDER

Borgo Press Books by S. Fowler Wright

THE ATTIC MURDER

AN INSPECTOR COMBRIDGE
AND MR. JELLIPOT
CLASSIC CRIME NOVEL

S. FOWLER WRIGHT

THE BORGO PRESS
MMXII

THE ATTIC MURDER

SECOND BORGO PRESS EDITION

Published by Wildside Press LLC

www.wildsidebooks.com

THE ATTIC MURDER

CONTENTS

CHAPTER ONE

"I'm afraid I can't give you references. I'm a stranger to London. Perhaps I'd better pay a week in advance?" His hand went boldly to his empty pocket. It was time he wanted—time at whatever cost. He could hear the police-whistles outside.

The old woman looked at him doubtfully. She had asked forty-five shillings, and would have taken half the amount.

"Have you got any luggage, Mr.—?" she began.

"Edwards," he answered. "Henry Edwards.... Yes. I shall bring my luggage this evening. Perhaps you could let me have some tea now, and a wash?"

He did not develop his proposal to pay in advance, and the old woman did not press it. He had a face and manner that inspired confidence. Had not Counsel for the Crown turned even this circumstance against him, and had not the soft-tongued Judge, with his tone of measured impartiality, supported the argument with a deadlier ingenuity? "You may regard the younger prisoner," he had said, "as having been under the influence of his more hardened companion. The impression which he will have made upon you while in the witness-box may not have been entirely unfavourable, even though, as men of the world—as men of common sense—you may observe the improbabilities of the tale he told you. But, if you are satisfied of his guilt, you must not allow such an impression to deflect your judgement, nor to cause you to forget the oaths you have taken. It is inevitable that men engaged in such crimes as that of which the prisoners are accused should be of sufficient address and plausibility to draw their intended victims into their clutches. The question of the prisoners' previous records (so far as they can be properly weighed against this class of criminality) will receive due and separate considerations, should you decide that their guilt is proved."

He had gone on to impress the jury with the gravity of the crime of which the confidence trickster is guilty, its increasing prevalence, and the reluctance of its victims to prosecute. All of which was true enough, but utterly irrelevant to the question of his guilt or innocence, and could only dispose the jury to convict him without too scrupulous weighing of the defence he had offered.

After hearing the summing-up, he had had no doubt of what that verdict would be. His most active resentment had been against the tone in which he had been told to stand up to hear the judgement delivered. Tony Welch had had five years. Well, he supposed he deserved it. And for him there had been fifteen months in the second division.

Before that, he had been asked whether he had any reason to offer why sentence should not be passed upon him. He knew that it was nothing more than a mockery of formula, but he had looked at the jury as he answered: "It only shows how useless it is to tell the truth," and he had seen one of them drop his eyes uncomfortably.

That had been an hour ago. Barely that. And then he had been hurried from the dock, and there had been a moment's confusion when the Inspector had knocked over the carafe in the room below, and—he had walked out. It had been as simple as that.

It must have been observed in five seconds, and his liberty would have been of the briefest, had he not noticed the street door standing unlatched, and the card APARTMENTS in the window, as he had turned the corner at a quick walk, which did not dare to seem hurried—and, at the moment's impulse, he had stepped inside and closed it.

No one had noticed. The street had been too full, and too busy.

He had stood in the little hall, after closing the door, and knocked on the table there, till the landlady had come up from the basement. "I couldn't make your bell ring, and the door was open," he had said pleasantly, and she had accepted his explanation without suspicion.

Half an hour later, he sat eating a stale egg, and drinking some ill-brewed tea, while he reviewed his position.

After all, it was largely his own fault, even apart from the impulsive folly which had involved him with Augusta Garten, and made him so maddeningly easy a catspaw in a game which he did not guess. He could, perhaps, have defended himself more easily had he given his own name, and enabled the police to establish an identity which would have made it at least improbable that he had been more than a recent and casual acquaintance of the major criminal. But the thought of Marian! His sister-in-law's outraged respectability, and his brother's jeers— no, he had been right to conceal it, at whatever cost.

But, that having been so, why should he not now go boldly back to his own identity? He considered the possibility only to discard it. There was the time of his absence, which would coincide so exactly with that during which he had been awaiting trial—above all, there were the fingerprints. What a fool he had been to allow them to be taken! But it had been done so suavely, and it was true that its first result had been to show that he was innocent of any previous charge.

It had seemed best not to object at the time—and now he had rendered his identification absolute and undeniable so long as his life should last, unless his hands should be lopped away. It was as though he walked the world with an indelible brand.... And he would always be a convicted criminal: always liable to be arrested and subjected to the unserved sentence: always liable to the blackmailing activities of any who should discover his identity.

Was there no way out? There were three, two of which he

was unwilling to face, and the third was a forlorn hope at best.

There was suicide. Always that. But to those who are young and healthy of mind it is a way that does not appeal; to those who have courage it is the way of cowardice and shame. He dismissed it at once. A theoretical road of escape, but one which he knew he would never take.

There was the way of submission. He might surrender himself to the blind omnipotence of the law, serve the sentence imposed, and return to his own identity with some invented excuse for his silent absence; and with at least something less to fear from exposure or blackmail than must be his lot while he continued to evade the penalty his conviction brought.

But he saw this also as an impossible choice. If he should be recaptured, he must submit to a power against which he had no strength to contend; but to do so by his own choice was beyond any resolution that he possessed. He had experienced too much already of the physical indignities, the degradations of enforced routines, which have substituted a spiritual persecution for the cruelties of neglect and dirt which were the prison horrors of a previous century. Beyond that, he had a natural, if somewhat illogical feeling, that to make such a surrender would be to accept the judgement of the court, as though he himself admitted guilt, and accepted the sentence which an impartial justice had imposed upon him.

The third road of escape was of a less sinister but more difficult character. He must obtain such evidence as would demonstrate his own innocence, and enable him to gain remission of the penalty. He knew too little of law to understand what obstacles of procedure there might be for one in such a position, already condemned, and avoiding the infliction of the allotted punishment; nor did his mind go so far ahead as to concern itself with such possibilities. The first part of such a programme presented sufficient difficulties for immediate consideration.

And, more urgent still, if he were to endeavour to obtain evidence that he were not the accomplice of organized fraud which twelve of his fellow citizens had declared him to be, he must consider how his immediate necessities could be supplied, and either this or another hiding-place be rendered permanently secure.

For the short moment he might be safe. Probably no one had seen him enter the house; and its proximity to the court would make it an unlikely place for the police to suspect. But there was no lasting comfort in this, when he considered the emptiness of his pockets, and that the luggage of which he had spoken would not arrive.

He had a well-founded fear that the police, being human, would give an amount of attention to such an escape disproportionate to any importance it might have to impartial eyes. It was certain that the assistance of the press would be invoked: that his description would be promptly circulated with the full and accurate details that the police cords would supply.

He had, of course, worn his own clothes in the dock. He was not embarrassed by prison garb. But there was little comfort in that while they could describe not only his appearance in every detail, but every garment that he had on. And he saw that, if he should go out after the next edition of evening papers had reached the street, not the police only, but every man he met, would be his potential foe.

In imagination, he ran from pursuing crowds; he heard police whistles rousing those ahead to obstruct his way; he jumped walls: he trod deeply in garden dirt; he was horribly cornered in cul-de-sacs; he crouched in corners, hearing voices that became louder with the sound of approaching feet.

And to avoid such ends he must think—think and plan—in the short hours of security that were his, while the search spread past him, and outward on every side. As he got up from the table, and moved to a fireside chair, leaving a well-cleared tray—for what certainty was there as to where or when his next meal would be?—he even had a faint transient smile for that abortive search on which he rightly guessed that so much energy was being wasted, while he had been taking a quiet meal almost within sight of the door out of which he walked.

CHAPTER TWO

As Francis Hammerton reflected thus, Mrs. Benson came in to clear.

He knew her name already from inspection of a business card that occupied a prominent position among the heterogeneous mantelpiece ornaments, and as he now parried questions to which accurate replies would have been of too startling a character, and assured himself with some difficulty that they were prompted by nothing more than a natural curiosity, he looked, with concealed anxiety, at the woman who might hold his fate in her hands in the next hour.

He supposed that she would be likely to indulge herself with an evening paper. It was less probable that she would go out to buy it. It would be pushed under her door. That might be any time now. Or she might prefer to have the final edition, two—even three—hours later than this.

If she should have it earlier, it might not be read till she had finished her washing up, and got other evening tasks off her mind. But, sooner or later, she would be certain to pick it up. Very soon she would see that headline: PRISONER ESCAPED FROM—. It was the kind of thing she would be certain to read. The financial news—the semi-final at Bolton—the trouble in Abyssinia—any of these she might be very likely to miss. But the escape of a prisoner in the next street! No, she would not overlook that.

Equally certain was it that she would guess who her new lodger was most likely to be. She would remember how he had let himself into the hall. She would calculate the time of his arrival, comparing it with that at which Harold Vaughan had escaped. She would read his description, and recognize some convincing detail.

Probably she might make excuse to come up, and refresh her memory, after which she would go or send to the police.

Should he give her time to do that? No, at the first sign of suspicion, he must make a quick bolt from the house. His over-excited imagination saw her obstructing him, attempting to hold him till the police should arrive. He struck at her clutching hands. He pushed her roughly away. She fell, and her head struck that sharp edge at the base of the table-leg, showing under the untidy table-cloth that drooped too far on this side. She lay still. He broke from the house, perhaps a hunted murderer now. She had to repeat her question of whether he would like macaroni for his evening meal, with a nice bit of plum-tart she had left over from the midday dinner, before he heard it....

He decided that she might not be a bad woman with whom to deal—almost certainly of a harmless type in normal circum-stances, but that if she guessed who he was she might betray him for half-a-crown.

Yet, was betrayal a fair word? He had come to her with a false name and a lying tale, and had bluffed her with a gesture of offering money he did not possess. And the crime of which he had been convicted was not of a pleasant kind.... No, he could not blame her should she decide that inclination and duty pointed in the same direction.

Then should he leave at once, before suspicion could be aroused? He debated this, after she had withdrawn from the room, and it appeared in no better light.

He would be penniless, shelterless, with the knowledge that every policeman he passed would be looking, with a sharp eye, for just such a one as himself; and that to apply for a lodging anywhere within walking distance would be to invite suspi-cion of who he was. And with no money—no luggage—what possible resort could he have that would avoid starvation, and would not lead to instant arrest?

Pondering thus, he resolved that the risks of the open street could not be less than those of the precarious shelter that he had found, and from this decision he saw further that he might have a better chance if he should himself reveal his identity, rather than to leave it to the almost certain discovery of the next hours.

By doing so, he could at least assert his innocence; could tell his tale, perhaps, so that it would rouse the sympathy of his auditor, and avoid the prejudice that his deception would naturally excite, should she learn of it by other means.

Deciding this, he had to consider what proposal he could make for discharging the cost of his lodging.

If he could win the woman's sympathy, he might remain there in almost absolute security, so long as he should not venture outside the door. And after a time he might walk boldly out, at least in the darker hours, trusting that the keenness of the first search would have relaxed, and that wherever it might be pursued, it would not be most active around the place of his conviction, with the immediate vicinity of which he had had no other connection, and to which it might seem particularly improbable that he would return.

But to remain in hiding thus would give him little opportunity of engaging in any occupation of a remunerative character. He could not hope for a sympathetic hearing if he should add to the fact that he was a convict dodging arrest a proposal that he should be fed and boarded free for an indefinite period, or until he should be recaptured by the police, and disappear for that which his sentence required.

This consideration naturally turned his thoughts to the money that was his, in his true name, and which he could obtain tomorrow by the simple process of cashing a cheque, if he should be prepared to face the risk of a walk through the streets, or of boarding a bus in the daylight hours, and of entering the bank, where he would be known, with the vague improbable risk that the police would have ascertained that Harold Vaughan and Francis Hammerton were the same, and be on the watch for him to enter so well-baited a trap.

He was not sure how he would attempt to reach it, but it was the thought of that available money that gave him courage for the present purpose he had in mind. He would tell the woman just how he was placed: would admit that he had lied about his luggage and other things. But he would add that he could get funds from his bank in the morning, and that he would then pay her in advance as he had first proposed; and she might well prefer, even if her sympathies remained unstirred, to take the money of so quietly-disposed a lodger, rather than have the barren satisfaction of turning him out.

Anyway, it could be tried, on the proverbial argument that a poor chance is better than none at all.... If he should be dissatisfied with her response, he would walk out at once to the street where already the twilight fell.... He need not delay to pack!

With these thoughts, being of a nature to challenge fate rather than dodge its blows, he went out to the hall and descended the basement stairs, down which he had heard Mrs. Benson's steps recede after she had cleared his table.

He was guided by the sound of a woman's voice along an ill-lighted passage to the door of her private retreat, and was about to knock when he was deterred by the words which he could clearly hear.

CHAPTER THREE

Francis Hammerton, if we are to think of him by his true name, had not considered the probability that Mrs. Benson might not be the sole occupant of the house, his mind having been concentrated upon aspects of his position which threatened more definite hazards.

Actually, the woman whose voice he heard was a next-door neighbour, Miss Janet Brown, who had looked in with no further purpose than to return a borrowed flat-iron. But it happened that she was already informed of the exciting incident of the afternoon, and when Mrs. Benson detained her for a cup of the tea which could be cheaply obtained by adding fresh water to the leaves in the lodger's teapot, and naturally mentioned the good fortune which had walked in less than two hours before, Janet was quick to see the connection between the events.

"Edwards?" she asked scornfully. "You call him Mr. Vaughan next time you go up, and see how he'll jump, or else answer his name without noticing how he's giving himself away, which would be just as good proof."

"I don't think I shall try that," Mrs. Benson answered doubtfully. She was sensibly trembling between the disappointment at the prospective loss of a most promising lodger, and vaguer fear of what so cunning and unscrupulous a character might be doing among the dowdy dining-room furniture. "I suppose," she concluded, "I'd better let the police know."

Miss Brown, a fair-haired angular woman, who showed her half-Scottish ancestry only in her bony figure, and the practical shrewdness with which she faced a difficult world, considered this proposition, and pronounced against it.

"There'll be a reward offered, if you wait, more like than not. It might be a hundred pounds! You'll be a fool if you let them know before that. Keep him close, I say, till you see how the cat jumps."

Mrs. Benson wavered miserably between the prospect of such wealth, and the shadow of a great fear. She was a woman who prided herself upon her respectability, which meant, among other things, that she came of a family who had no dealings with the police.

Even for a criminal to be arrested beneath her roof would tend to taint her with the stigma of an undesired and undesirable notoriety. It was not at all the kind of thing which her deceased parents would have approved. It might not be quite so disgraceful as being behind with the rent (which had actually happened three years ago, though, by the combined mercies of Heaven and Mr. Clay, it was known to none but herself and the landlord's agent), but it was not the kind of thing that should occur in the house of a woman whose uncle was a builder's merchant, and whose brother-in-law had once sat on a Rural District Council.

But, far worse than that, suppose that, by not giving information at once, she should "get in trouble" with the police.

"I don't know," she said, "what I ought to do. Not rightly. He might clear off before then."

The last sentence was spoken in a tone between hope and fear. Had she heard the front door bang at that moment, her first sensation might have been relief, rather than regret for a lodger lost, or the romantic shadow of reward faded away.

But Miss Brown put the suggestion aside. "Not he," she said. "If you don't let him see you suspect. He'll be lying too snug for that.... You'll find he won't stir out of the door, more likely than not.... You can just wait till the reward comes out, and walk round the corner to pick it up."

"Suppose they say I ought to have told them before?"

"Told them what? Your lodger's a different name, isn't he? How can you tell that as you don't know? Even then, you won't do more than a guess.

"You don't read the papers much. You're too busy for that, with all our lodgers to feed, and to wash and mend, and the house cleaning from attic down.... But you see the bills. £100 REWARD! Anyone'd stop to read them—and you go straight round on the chance."

Francis Hammerton, having heard the most part of this conversation, or at least Janet's part in it, for Mrs. Benson had a voice of less penetrating quality, did not wait to hear more.

He had heard sufficient to conclude that he would not be immediately denounced, and to see that he would increase his peril by confessing an identity already guessed. Janet's last statement led him to conclude that there were most probably other lodgers in the house, and he saw that this must increase the risk of discovery while he remained listening at Mrs. Benson's door.

Even in a less compromising position, he would have had no inclination to make himself known to the other occupants of the house, or to give occasion for his presence to be narrated to them. He went back while he safely could.

CHAPTER FOUR

With some trepidation, only partially controlled, Mrs. Benson brought up the supper.

It was a condition of which her lodger might have been less observant had he not already heard the suspicions which had been suggested to her. He had resolved that he would say nothing to confirm them, but rather aim to confuse her with a doubt as to whether her neighbour's accusation might be no more than a baseless guess, and he was therefore careful to give no sign of observing her agitation. He talked in a casual manner of trivial indifferent things, as one who had the leisure of an unoccupied mind.

The evening had turned wet as the dusk fell, and now the rattling of the ill-fitting window-frame, and the beat of heavy rain on the glass, gave him a good excuse as he said: "I don't think I'll go out to fetch my luggage tonight, Mrs. Benson, if you don't mind.... I shall have to go to the bank in the morning, and I can do everything at the same time.... I daresay I can manage somehow till then.... And I'll settle up tomorrow for the first week We're strangers to one another as yet, so I'd rather have it that way, though I hope you'll get to know me better before long."

Mrs. Benson was flutteringly acquiescent in her replies. "Yes, sir. It's for you to say, sir.... Yes, sir. I hope you will. If there's anything that I could do. Would you like the paper, sir, if as how you'll be sitting quiet? There's no one else coming in tonight till the last thing.... Yes, sir, thank you. I wouldn't ask, but the truth is I've been doing that bad since Mr. Michaelson left.... But I'll bring it up if you'll be wanting something to read."

The last offer, which had had its birth in Janet Brown's livelier brain, was brought out, and repeated, in nervous haste, like a lesson learned. But Mr. Edwards still appeared to notice nothing strange in his landlady's manners or speech. He said pleasantly that he should like to see it, if it wouldn't be robbing her. And when she came up, half an hour later, to clear the table, and bringing the final edition of the *Evening News*, he restrained the half-fearful desire he had to see the published account of his trial and subsequent escape, turning to the sporting page in a desultory manner, until the table was cleared, and she had left the room.

The report itself was not long, the detailed interest of the case having been the news of the previous day, when the evidence had been heard. It consisted mainly of a skilfully condensed summary of the Judge's address to the jury, the time during which they had been absent from court, and other similar details with which he was already too familiar to give them more than one swift comprehending glance, which went on to where, in bolder type, was the news of his own escape.

It gave him a thrill of exaltation, overcoming for one brief moment the misery that possessed his mind, to realize the extent and energy of the futile search which was being made while he remained within two hundred yards of the headquarters of the baffled power of the law.

But the feeling changed to a greater depression with realization of the desperation of his position, as he went on to read the accurate description of himself which the police had been prompt to communicate to the Press.

He saw a portrait also, which might have been more exact had the artist not thought it necessary to give him a cunningly ingratiating expression, less natural to himself than to the character which the jury's verdict had fixed upon him.

But for that overheard conversation, he would have walked out at once, trusting to darkness and rain, and regardless of all beside under the urgent fear that the hunted have. As it was, he wondered with what object the newspaper had been brought. If it had been meant as a test, he thought that his demeanour must have puzzled the woman, though, with that detailed description to support suspicion already formed, it could hardly have had a more negative result.

Was it possible that it had been brought up in simplicity and goodwill, without previous reading of the exposure which it contained? Remembering what he had heard, he put the idea aside. The improbability was too great.

But the issue of all his doubts was to resolve that it would be a less risk to remain in his present quarters till morning came than to wander penniless in the rain through the midnight hours.

He went up to a better bed than the jail authorities would have provided, with little expectation that sleep would be quick to come, and was conscious of nothing more till he saw the light of the winter dawn invading a dingy room.

CHAPTER FIVE

It must be eight o'clock by the growing light. It was time to rise. But there was no instant hurry for that. Let him think first. He might have been commencing his first day as a convict now, with no option as to the hour when he must leave his bed!

That was something gained, though there might be penalties in the opposite scale when he should be caught, which he recognized, in the clear light of thought that the morning gives, to be the most probable end.

But meanwhile there was a precarious haven, even in the shabbiness of this unwashed room, where he could lie for the time he would.... Perhaps only till there should come the sound of heavy feet on the stairs, and he would be ignominiously conducted back to the servitude he had sought to dodge.... There was such a foot on the stair now.

But it was going down, not up. It receded, and there was silence again. Was he a fool to stay longer here? Would it not be well to have breakfast and go while he still could? In the open street he would be less easy to catch.

He considered, for the first time, that his recent associates would have read the tale of his escape, and might anticipate that he would be coming to them for help. He was not sure what reception he would get, but he saw danger in the attempt, for it was in that direction that the police would be most alert, and the meshes of the net would be very small. It was exactly there that he must not go. Perhaps his best chance of escape lay in the fact that he was not really one of the gang, and that he had resources in a direction which he still felt some confidence that the police did not suspect....

Yet, if he were to keep distant from those resorts, how did he suppose that he could obtain evidence through which his own innocence could be proved...? Augusta Garten would know that he had got free. He would have liked to see her again. To have reproached her with all the bitterness of the love abused that had brought him here. To see the shame—or would it be ridicule?—in her eyes. But not to ask help from her. Never that.

Yet money he must have, without which, or the help of friends, he saw that his chance of prolonged freedom was small indeed. It must be got from his own bank, and it would be best to walk in there without having the appearance of a man who had spent the night on the streets.... A razor he must certainly get.... Unless, of course, he should prefer to disguise himself with a growth of beard. That might be a good idea, but it was a form of camouflage which required time to bring it to perfect flower. He supposed that a two or three days' growth would attract notice rather than cause him to be overlooked, and though he was vague in guessing how long a respectable beard would take to grow, or how soon a reward for an escaped prisoner might be announced, he had a sound suspicion that the second period might be the shorter.

But a razor was not an article which Mrs. Benson would be likely to have in readiness to lend at her lodgers' needs, nor was it likely that she would consent to borrow it for him from the room of the overhead lodger whose step he had heard as he left the house.

He was half dressed by this time, and opened his door on to a small square of landing from which narrow stairs descended to the ground floor, and others, narrower still, mounted to attic rooms.

There was no sound. Probably Mrs. Benson was in the basement. There might be no others in the house. It could be done at a small risk. If he were challenged, he would tell the truth. He sought to borrow a razor which he unfortunately lacked till his luggage should have arrived. Very quietly, he mounted the stairs.

He came to an uncarpeted landing, which had a closed door upon either side. It was lit by a skylight in the sloping roof, the lowness of which suggested that the rooms could not be let to any but impecunious tenants. Doubtless, the one was occupied by the man whose heavy descending step he had heard, and the other, most probably, by Mrs. Benson herself. If so, it was unlikely that he would be disturbed, for the woman would not be in her bedroom during the breakfast hour.

With nothing but chance to direct his choice, he approached the left-hand door, and knocked. As he had expected, there was no reply, and he turned the handle boldly, to discover that he was faced by a locked door.

The next moment, he heard a girl's voice: "Is that you, Mrs. Benson?"

The voice had a timid uncertain sound, and he stood for a moment in hesitation as to whether he should reply, and, while he did so, she spoke again. "It's no use waiting here. I shan't be up for hours yet. I thought you'd gone." And then, in a firmer tone: "It's no use waiting, I tell you. You'd better go. I shan't unlock the door till Mrs. Benson comes up."

The words gave him a simple clue. It was evident that he was supposed to be the occupant of the opposite room. If so, what more natural than that he should return to it after this rebuff? What more satisfactory than to know that the other would remain locked until he should be heard to descend, apart from the unlikely chance that the landlady would promptly appear?

Treading loudly now on the bare boards, he took the two strides that the narrow landing required, and had the satisfaction of opening an unlocked door, and looking round on an empty room.

It was low-ceiled, as he had expected to see, and lighted only by a dormer window, but its appearance was surprising in other ways. It was evident, even to his first hurried glance, that, though the furnishing of the room was of the kind which might have been anticipated by one who had become familiar with the lower parts of the house, it contained the possessions of a man who did not dress or live in a mean way. Even the quality of the cabin-trunk, which was too large to be pushed close to the low wall of the slant-roofed attic, and must have been difficult to get up the narrow twisting stairs, was incongruous to the setting in which it stood.

But it was an incongruity of which Francis Hammerton was only subconsciously aware, having more urgent interests to engage his mind. He saw a shaving-glass on the wall, and, beneath it, the safety-razor he sought. A minute later, he was back in his own room, not without a feeling of satisfaction in the success of this minor operation of the criminal character which had been thrust upon him. But there was a new doubt now in his mind of whether he should venture upstairs again to return the borrowed article as soon as he had finished its present use, or trust to the chance of a later hour, or the probability that he would have left the house before discovery of that petty pilfering would be made.

Finally, he decided to return it at once, which he did apparently without observation, and went down to the room in which he had had his meals during the previous day, his mind being now made up that he would leave the house as soon as he had eaten the breakfast which his empty pockets could procure in no other place.

To call at his own bank might be hazardous, but it was a risk he could not avoid, and, if it were to be done at all, it could not be tried too soon.

He saw that, in view of the suspicion with which he was regarded by his landlady, and the plan he had overheard, he must walk out in such a way that she would not doubt that he would return. He must either leave his bill permanently unpaid, or incur the risk of a subsequent communication, with the probability that he might be arrested in the meantime, in which case he could not tell what facilities would be permitted him for discharging the debt.

He saw, as he thought of this, and of the lies he had told already, and of the purpose that had taken him to the attic rooms, how hard it may be for one who has been labelled criminal by the law to avoid the character which is placed upon him. Whatever he be at first, he may be forced to the incidence of a life of crime.... His mind returned to more practical considerations as he entered the room, and perceived that breakfast was laid for two.

His step, being audible to Mrs. Benson in her basement room, was sufficient signal to bring her up with a pot of tea, more or less fresh, and a plate of quite decent bacon, which she laid on the table with a remark that Miss Jones ought to have been down before this. She supposed that she must have overslept.

Francis recalled the conversation by which he had secured asylum on the previous afternoon, and recognized that he had not been promised exclusive occupation of the room. It had been assumed by him, rather than said by her, and his position had not been favourable to a critical examination of the nature of the lodging, with partial board, for which Mrs. Benson had quoted. But he saw that if he were expected to take his breakfast (included in the quoted figure), or other meals (which would be extras), under the observation of others who would be able to compare him at close quarters with the descriptions which the morning newspapers would supply, it was an additional reason why his departure should not delay.

With these thoughts at the back of his mind, he answered Mrs. Benson's remark as casually as it had been made: "Perhaps she won't be long. I'm afraid I'm rather late myself."

He glanced at a massive mantelpiece clock, the hands of which pointed to twenty minutes to nine. Her eyes followed his, and she said: "You mustn't go by that. It's half an hour slow, if not more."

She pulled a chair up to the table for him, and he sat down as he replied: "It doesn't really matter to me. I don't think the bank opens before ten."

"I'd better see if Miss Jones is up now," Mrs. Benson replied, inconsequently, with a note of irritation in her voice. It was an hour at which she expected to have her breakfasts cleared away, and her washing-up done.

He saw that a newspaper lay on the table with an appearance of not having been opened. "I suppose that is Miss Jones' paper?" he asked, as the woman was about to withdraw. If it were one that was free to the lodgers generally, he would much prefer to have it in his own hands before the lady's arrival. Probably it would have another of those infernal portraits! But he doubted that Mrs. Benson would make such provision for her guests.

"No, sir. That's Mr. Rabone's, but he doesn't look at it, more mornings than not."

"And I suppose he's another one who's rather late this morning?"

"No, sir. He's gone before now. He always leaves before this." She went out as she replied, and he heard her ascending the creaking stairs.

He picked up the paper, but did not turn to the account of his own conviction, or subsequent escape. He had seen enough in the *Evening News* concerning a matter on which he knew more than he was likely to read. Nor did he need to be informed that the criminal was still "at large," as it would be certain to state. It would be better that Miss Jones, if she were of an observant disposition, should see him reading the sporting news, or studying the exchanges of the previous day.

Supposing it to be the etiquette of the table that each lodger should settle to his own meal without reference to other comers, he commenced his breakfast, observing, as he did so, that he sat facing a window the side-curtains of which did not exclude the observation of those who passed in the street, though, the room being on a slightly higher level, it might be no more than his head which would be visible to anyone of average height. Suppose that a policeman, strolling along, and occupied only in observation of the potential criminals on his beat— The fact that the rain was descending steadily made such leisurely observation unlikely, but offered another trouble to his harassed mind. He had neither umbrella nor other covering from the weather. He neither desired to be soaked, nor to enter the bank with the appearance of a half-drowned fowl.

It was possible that Mr. Rabone had left a spare overcoat in his room, but there was little doubt as to what Mrs. Benson's reaction would be if she should meet her new lodger on the stairs with such a garment upon him.... It seemed that it would be necessary to wait for the rain to cease.

He was still considering this problem when Miss Jones entered the room.

CHAPTER SIX

His eyes met those of a girl who was young, slim, dark, and of so self-possessed a manner that he had a moment's doubt of whether it could be she whose voice he had heard through the attic door.

But when she spoke he recognized it as the same, though it was without any trace of the timidity which he had noticed before.

"Mrs. Benson told me that she had a new guest. I must introduce myself. I am Mary Jones."

"It is pleasant to have company," he answered, with more sincerity than he had expected to feel. "I thought I should be alone. My name is—" There was a second's hesitation as his thought paused for the selection of the right lie, the instinct to give his true name being confused between the two others that he had subsequently assumed; but he did not think it to be observed, her interruption came so quickly: "Oh, yes. Mrs. Benson told me your name."

Mr. Edwards, as he concluded that he had become to her, having risen to draw out the lady's chair, which was at the side of the table facing the door, at right angles to his own, sat down again, sensible of the attractions of his breakfast companion, but most conscious of the need for that constant watchfulness which is common to most creatures which live in lasting peril of death should their wits relax, but from which civilized man, and some of his domesticated companions, have become normally free. Beneath this instinct there was another, subconsciously strong, urging him to make any friend he could from among those who had become his collective foes. It led him to lay down the newspaper, though with some reluctance, for he had realized its value in hiding him from the eyes of those who passed in the street.

He talked for a time, as the meal progressed, of trivial or indifferent things, but not without realizing how difficult it was, even in such conversation as that, to avoid self-revealing references to past environment or experience; and with his abnormally sensitive perceptions troubled by a feeling that the girl was concentrating her observation upon him with what he felt to be an abnormal intensity.

He thought he had the explanation of that, when she asked him, with a cool and smiling deliberation: "Mr. Edwards, do you mind telling me why you knocked at my door this morning?"

He found the truth to be the easiest, as it was certainly the wisest reply: "I wanted to borrow a razor."

"And you got it from Mr. Rabone's room?"

"Yes," he said. "So I did. And returned it afterwards."

She was silent for a moment, after which she looked at him in a more friendly intimate way than she had done previously. She asked: "Mr. Edwards, should you think it impertinent if I were to give you a word of advice?"

"No. I should be grateful."

"I shouldn't mention to Mr. Rabone, if I were you, that you went into his room."

She spoke with a seriousness that seemed more than the incident could deserve, and he recalled the words that he had heard through the door when she had supposed that it was his fellow-lodger to whom she spoke.

"You don't like Mr. Rabone?" he ventured.

Her reply paused. Then she said seriously: "You must please not conclude that. I trust you to respect my confidence when I say no more nor less than that I should be sorry for any stranger whom he might suspect of poking about his room."

"Yet he leaves it unlocked?"

"I don't suppose he minds Mrs. Benson putting it straight.

That's a very different thing."

"Well," he said, "thanks for the hint. I'm not likely to go there again." He considered that he had more serious troubles than a borrowed razor was likely to stir, but he appreciated the friendly spirit in which the caution was given. He said: "I don't see that there'll be any occasion to mention it, as I put it back. For that matter, I mayn't be here when he returns."

He was pleased to see, or imagine, a shadow of annoyance if not regret on the girl's face as she heard that. It strengthened an impulse to give her fuller confidence, which may have sprung in part from natural desire for any friendship he could make, in the loneliness of the life which must now be his.

"Then you're not staying," she asked, "after today?"

"I don't quite know what I shall do."

He thought, as he had done before, that he saw curiosity in her eyes, beyond reason toward one whom she had met in so casual a way. Could it be that she suspected the truth?

He doubted that, but felt an instinctive desire to tell it; to gain a confidante who, he felt sure, would not betray him, even for a reward. But if she did not herself betray, she might talk. His liberty would not be long if he should reveal his identity to every stranger he met.

"I'm sorry you're not likely to stay," she said; "we could do with someone else here."

"You are here permanently yourself?"

"I don't know any more than you seem to. At present, I'm looking for work that I can't get."

It was then that a wild vague thought entered his mind that she might be one who would share his fortunes, who would help him (for a consideration, of course) in the delicate operation of drawing the money from his bank for which it might be so dangerous to apply, and was yet so vital to have. Perhaps even to spend it with him on a more permanent basis to help him to a new identity: to assist in rebuilding all that had seemed so utterly lost.

But, as he looked at her, he did not feel it to be a plan to which she would be likely to conform in a docile way. He had sufficient detachment of mind to see it as an idea which would not have come to him in more normal circumstances. But the instinct to confide in those around him, to gain allies if he could, which had taken him down to Mrs. Benson's kitchen the night before, urged him again, and in greater confidence than he had then felt. And he saw that his decision must be promptly made, or the opportunity might be gone. The meal was done. Any moment she might rise and disappear for ever out of his life.

"Miss Jones," he asked, with a nervousness in his voice she had not noticed before, "have you anything very urgent to do this morning?"

She looked a natural surprise, but answered simply: "No. Why do you want to know?"

"I wondered whether I might ask you to do something for me. Of course, I'd pay for your time." He added, as though in self-defence: "It was you saying you were looking out for a job that put it into my mind."

"So I am. It depends upon what it is that you want me to do."

"It's only to go to the bank for me, but there's something that I should have to explain first."

"I don't see why I should refuse that. But I'm an utter stranger to you. I think I ought to explain too. I'm out of work, and my money's just about gone. Mr. Rabone might happen to tell you that.... So," she concluded with a smile, "you mustn't tempt me too far."

"I shouldn't worry much about that.... Could you believe that anyone could be convicted of a very serious crime, and not be guilty at all?"

"Yes, I could believe that; though I don't think it often happens.... But don't you think you'd better ring the bell first— it's the one on the left, the other's a dud—and let Mrs. Benson clear away before you tell me what you want me to do...? I've got a few things to see to upstairs before I could go out."

With these words, Miss Jones rose and left the room. He saw the wisdom of deferring the tale he had to tell until their landlady should have cleared away, and withdrawn from the scene. He recognized the easy efficiency with which Miss Jones handled the situation, and the difficulty of reconciling this character with the words and tone which he had heard through the attic door recurred to his mind.

Who could this Rabone be, and why, though he appeared to be one whom she both feared and disliked, should she have confided to him that her money was nearly gone? He felt an active dislike for the man with whose razor he had made acquaintance, though he knew him only as a heavy step on the stair. If the girl were being persecuted or molested by him, the law was surely equal to her protection! Single girls should be secure in their lodgings from molestation by fellow-boarders of habits and manners as execrable as he had doubt that those of Mr. Rabone would prove to be.... The law? He saw that it was not a drama in which he could be cast for a leading part.

CHAPTER SEVEN

It was half an hour later when Miss Jones re-entered the room. She did not come near the fire, but sat down at the farther side of the table, as though desiring that a formal distance should be maintained. "I've been thinking over," she began, "what you said, and I thought at first I'd rather you didn't tell me more than was necessary for what you want me to do, because we're really strangers to one another, and mayn't meet again, for all we know, after today. But I've thought since that you ought to be the best judge, as you know what it is, and I don't; and the more I know the less likely I shall be to put my foot in it, so I'll just leave it to you."

"I've been thinking it over too," he replied, "and it's clear to me that I can't ask you to do anything till I've fully explained. Apart from other reasons, it wouldn't be fair to you. And if— anything—were to happen, I should like to feel that there's someone who knows what the truth is."

"Very well," she said. "Fire away. Anyhow, I shouldn't want to go out in this rain. It seems to be getting worse all the time." She sat with her elbows on the table, and her chin in her hands, as she listened to the tale that he had to tell.

"I suppose," he said, as it concluded, "it makes me sound rather a fool. It's just a question of fool or knave, and the less there is of the one, the more the other comes up. The jury must have seen that, and they may have thought I'd tried to make myself out a bigger fool than anyone was likely to be.

"But you can see that there were some things that I couldn't tell. I should think that that often happens, and people have to let things that they did sound worse than they really were."

"Yes," she answered, "perhaps it may. But I should think the jury were rather fools too."

The remark, noncommittal as it was, gave him a new confidence, with the conviction that she believed his tale. He added: "You see I hadn't even meant to use any name but my own. It wouldn't have come into my mind. I only went there at all because Bob Powell said that if we didn't finish up with a night-club it wouldn't be worth calling a night at all. But then, when we got in, he said that there were some people there who didn't know him by sight, but would know his name, and be certain to tell his wife, and he called himself something that I forget, and introduced me as Harold Vaughan.... And I don't know whether Tony ever doubted that it was my own name, though that's hard to say. But I feel sure that Augusta didn't, and it was for her sake that I kept in with the gang.

"And what part she had in it herself I don't know even now, but I'm glad she didn't get hauled into the dock, though I can't say that I ever want to see her again. But it's a fact that till I was arrested I'd never guessed what the game was.

"It sounds silly now, but if I'd met Tony, it would be easier to understand. He could talk the leg off a chair in his plausible smiling way.... And not guessing anything must have made me twice the value to him.... But I couldn't say how I met him, and came to be using another name, without it all coming out who I really was, beside giving Bob Powell away."

"Yes," she answered doubtfully. "I think I see how you felt, though it doesn't sound much of a reason when you look at what a mess you're in now. And the fact that they couldn't find out who you were, that you had no background that they could check up—the judge would know that, even though it mightn't be allowed to come to the jury's ears—would prejudice everyone against you, and make it seem certain that you were one of the gang.... But the question is, what do you want me to do now?"

"I've got money in my own bank, which I'm bound to get

hold of. I thought, to begin with, I might give you a note to the bank, asking for a cheque-book. They'd know my signature, and wouldn't be likely to ask any questions about that. It wouldn't be exactly like drawing money, and even that they'd have no right to raise any difficulty about."

"No. Not exactly the same. But I suppose you'd want me to draw the money out a few hours later?"

The tone was noncommittal, if nothing worse. He became aware that he might have to face refusal of his request. But he could not deny that his programme would involve a second call at the bank, and one that should be made very promptly after the first. He said: "You see, I haven't got a penny till I can get a cheque cashed. And I don't want to stay here longer than I'm obliged."

She turned the conversation to ask: "Any special reason for that? You don't think anyone saw you come in?"

"No. It's a different reason." He hesitated a moment. Was he being as utter a fool as Tony Welch had made him before? But he had the sense to see that he had gone too far for a safe retreat: that to give her a doubt as to whether he were being entirely frank would be worse than to have said nothing at all. After that momentary hesitation, he narrated the conversation that he had overheard the evening before.

"It does make it a bit awkward," she said thoughtfully. "I was going to suggest that you might stay here safely for a few days, if you could keep out of Mr. Rabone's way, and in that time I might get you the money by other means, if you'd trust me enough for that. I don't know much about how soon they offer rewards for escaped prisoners, nor whether they do it at all, but I shouldn't think there'd be any rush to begin. But if the woman next door's got the idea, she's more likely to talk than not, and— well, it's not raining much now, so if you'll write the note while I'm upstairs, I'll get ready to go." He had to ask for further assistance, having neither paper nor pen, but she was soon ready, and armed with a note from Francis Hammerton, headed with his private address, and requesting his bankers to provide him with a book containing twenty-four uncrossed cheques, and to charge it to his account.

"If I'm not back," she said, "in the next hour, you'll know that something's happened at the bank which makes me think it's not safe. In that case, you must trust me to come back, or find some other means of letting you know, as soon as I safely can."

"But," he protested, with the fuller realization of what he was asking her to risk and do which her words brought, "I couldn't ask you to do that. How would you—?"

She interrupted him to reply: "I only said *if.* I don't expect there'll be any trouble at all. I just wanted you to understand that if I'm not back in an hour, it won't mean that I'm forging cheques all over the place. I expect the bank will hand it out without giving me more than a look. Why shouldn't they? There doesn't seem to be anyone but this Bob Powell you mention who could connect you with your real name, and you'd have heard before now if he'd let that out, and in a different way."

She turned to go, and then hesitated, as though having something further to say. But then she thought: "I don't suppose, if I told him, that it would enable him to get clear in time."

She had a second impulse that came near to speech, but checked herself again with the thought: "Well, if that happened, he'd find out soon enough; and it would mean explaining a lot if I said it now." She repeated: "I don't suppose I shall be more than an hour," and went out.

She left him puzzled in mind, but feeling that he had been fortunate in gaining a friend at so great a need.

CHAPTER EIGHT

Francis became more nervous of the window as the rain ceased and the light improved. He would not retire to his own room, being alert by that time for the girl's return, but he sat by the fire in what he thought would be a natural pose to the eyes of anyone who might glance in, and which kept his face hidden behind the pages of the *Daily Record*. Doing this, he found after a time that it required an effort of will to move the paper away, lest his eyes should confront those of some suspicious officer of the law gazing in from the street upon a lodger whom Mrs. Benson had acquired during the previous day.

He told himself irritably that he was a damnable coward, and that it would be better to give himself up at once than to allow his fears to make a purgatory of every hour of the day. But he defended himself from his own contempt with the argument that his empty pockets, and the inaction that they entailed, were responsible for these nervous fears that reason would not control. If he could be active on his own behalf—how soon would she be back?

He calculated the time which the journey would require. With all allowances, even to an imagined crowd at the bank counter, it should be done in an hour. He could not make it longer than that.

But the hour passed, and a half-hour beyond, and she did not come. He must conclude, from her own assurance, that this delay was a sign either that she had been detained or followed, which stirred him to a new fear.

Would she be sufficiently skilful to dodge pursuit, or would she be traced by those whom his own folly would have guided to his retreat? Or was she now being detained and questioned with a severity which she could not indefinitely sustain? Or, perhaps, herself under some charge which his own knowledge of law was not sufficient to formulate to his own fears, as having applied for a cheque-book without being able or willing to give a proper account of how she came to be sent on such an errand? Could he reasonably expect that she would sustain such an inquisition for one who had given her such casual employment, and had been a stranger to her three hours before?

While he tried to control these impatient doubts, Mrs. Benson appeared to spread a cloth for the midday meal. He thought she looked at him in a sour way, as though she hesitated on the edge of saying things which he would not be pleased to hear, or asking questions to which it might not be easy to find reply.

It was an attitude simple to understand, she thinking him to be what he was, or even something worse, and he having assured her that he was going out to draw money, which he had made no motion to do.

He could have said that Miss Jones had kindly consented to call at the bank on his behalf, but he doubted the wisdom of that till he knew what the result of her adventure was. But would his silence annoy the woman into denouncing him to the police without waiting for the precarious chance of a reward which must be weighed against the certainty that she was feeding a lodger who did not pay? Would she conclude that his talk of a bank was no more than the ready tale of one who was practised in abusing the confidence of others as his conviction indicated?

Vexed by these thoughts, to which no satisfactory answers appeared, he did not venture even to look directly at her, lest he should encourage the asking of questions to which he had no reply, and the attitude of dejection and anxiety which she observed actually had a different effect on her mind from that which his fears supposed.

In fact, her vague horror of criminality, in whatever form,

was not entirely proof against actual contact with one who, to the instincts by which those of undeveloped mentality are largely accustomed to rule their lives, did not appear to be of a repellent or hostile type.

When she did speak, it was only to ask, as she laid for three on the dingy cloth: "I suppose Miss Jones didn't happen to say whether she'd be coming in? She mostly does, or let's me know if she won't."

"No," he said, with some hesitation, wishing neither to show what he knew, nor to be inconsistent with anything that Miss Jones might say on her return, "she might come in any time, as far as I understood."

"There'll be Mr. Rabone, anyway," the woman went on. "He said he'd be coming in, as he doesn't do most days, not before-night." She added, in a grumbling undertone: "I suppose my dinners aren't good enough for the likes of him." And then, in a more audible voice, but still in the tone of one who had a developed habit of muttering aloud, rather than conversing with others: "Not as she'd be more likely to come in for that."

As she spoke, there was the sound of a latchkey in the street-door, and the heavy step of the top-floor lodger sounded along the passage, and up the thinly-carpeted stairs.

Francis Hammerton restrained a prudent or cowardly impulse to rise and withdraw to his own room. He had to face the difficulty of securing solitude in a crowded city, which is particularly great for one whose pockets are bare. Two minutes later, the opportunity had gone. William Rabone entered the room.

Mrs. Benson, taking his appearance as a signal that the meal should be served, without longer waiting for her female lodger, had retreated to the kitchen to dish it up, and Francis was spared an introduction he did not desire.

The man who entered was dark, large, heavily built, and of professional rather than commercial aspect, in spite of the absurd toothbrush on his upper lip, which appeared to under-study either Charlie Chaplin or the German Chancellor.

He looked at Francis with unconcealed annoyance, for which

there may have been sufficient reason in the fact that he had anticipated the presence of Mary Jones, and that she would be his sole company at the meal.

But this first glance was casual in its hostility. The second was more intent.

"Good morning, Mr. Vaughan," he said, with some stress on the final word. Francis looked at him with an expression which he intended for indifferent surprise. "My name is Edwards."

"Glad to know.... I expect you think it's best not to go out in this weather."

Francis was spared the necessity of reply by the arrival of Mrs. Benson with a tray bearing a boiled neck of mutton, and two dishes of vegetables; and before she retired, Mary Jones had also entered, and taken her seat at the table.

Miss Jones said nothing, nor did she look at either of her fellow-guests, settling herself to her own meal as indifferently as though she were the only one there.

It appeared that it was a table at which no one presided, its etiquette being that the dishes were passed or pushed toward each diner in turn, for the satisfaction of their own requirements. Jones accepted these services with monosyllabic thanks to those in whose existence she seemed otherwise uninterested.

Conversation was slow to commence among three people who were alike in feeling that they were one too many, though they would have differed as to the one whose presence was not required.

Mr. Rabone, who preferred better meals than Mrs. Benson provided, had come in with the sole object of indulging in the society of Miss Jones in a manner inappropriate to the presence of a third party: Francis had even more urgent, if not more important reason for wishing to talk to that lady alone: Mary Jones had a report to make which was not for Mr. Rabone's ears. She also would have preferred that Francis should have been alone when she arrived, but, as Rabone was there, she had a modified satisfaction in the fact that she was not singly with him. But she told herself that this was mere cowardice, by which she thanked fate for postponing that which she had been active to bring about.

The neck of mutton had been succeeded by apple-dumplings when Rabone addressed Miss Jones in a direct and serious way. His question was blunt to the edge of rudeness: "Shall you be going out this afternoon?"

Her reply hesitated, as though the question were an embarrassment, and when she replied it was indirectly, and with a timidity of tone and manner very different from that in which she had conversed with Francis during the morning, and which reminded him again of the voice which he had first heard through the attic door. She said: "I expect I shall be in this evening."

Mr. Rabone considered this reply, on which he made no comment to her, but he looked at Francis to ask, in a manner which was more a direction than a request: "You will be going out after dark?"

Francis restrained himself to answer: "Perhaps I shall."

Mr. Rabone said no more until the meal ended, and Miss Jones had risen and silently left the room. Then he turned to Francis with unfriendly and somewhat contemptuous eyes. "Staying here?" he asked curtly.

"I may."

"I think not."

Francis made no answer to that. He saw that those who recognized him were now in a position to move him on, as a policeman deals with a tramp. But without money—without having the girl's report of the errand in which she had so probably failed—

Mr. Rabone spoke again: "Can you give me change for ten shillings?"

"Not at the moment."

"So I supposed." He pulled out a pocket-book fat with notes. Evidently it was not poverty which caused him to choose that modest, if respectable lodging.

He took out a pound-note, hesitated between that and one for half the amount, and finally selected two of ten shillings each, which he passed across the table.

Francis looked at the money, letting it lie. The action was generous in itself, but it was evidently without goodwill. Its manner made it an insult, very hard not to refuse.

But suppose that the girl had failed, as her delay in returning appeared to indicate? Suppose that she were waiting now for the opportunity to tell him quietly that he could not be too speedy to leave? There might be freedom in those two slips of coloured paper so contemptuously tossed over the cloth. There would surely be rest and food at an urgent need

Anyway, he must learn to obey the orders of all men who could address him as Harold Vaughan, even though they offered no money to enforce their wills.

He picked it up with a conventional word of thanks which did attempt pretence of gratitude, as for a friend's aid, nor that he was in less than an utter need. He said: "We will call it a loan. You shall have it back during the next few days."

"Call it what you will. You must be gone from here when I get back. That's at six tonight."

He rose, and went up to his room. Ten minutes later Francis heard him leave, and almost immediately after Miss Jones came down.

She had her bag in her hand, from which she drew the cheque-book that he required.

"Was it all right?" he asked. "I was afraid when you didn't get back—"

"I think so, but I'm not sure. I went to a cashier who was not occupied when I got to the counter, and gave him the note. He was reading it when another customer came up. The cashier looked at him, and then said to me: "Just a moment, please," and went to the back.

"I thought I should have some trouble to face, but when he returned he just gave me the book in the usual way. The man who came after me had pushed a cheque over to him for payment, and I looked back as I went out of the door, and the cashier wasn't paying it, but talking to him, with it in his hand.

"That looked as though he had gone behind to enquire something about him rather than me, when he first saw him come up, without wishing to do it so that he would be understood—perhaps to see what his balance was—and I felt easy; but after that I got an idea that I was being followed. It may have been only nervousness, but I went a good way round, to make sure."

"You are sure?"

"Yes. I mean I'm sure no one followed me here."

Francis noticed the quiet confidence in her voice, and that she had been sufficiently conversant with banking methods to judge what had occurred in a cool and probable way. He asked: "You won't mind going again? There'll be just about time before they close."

She did not refuse, but neither did she agree. She said:

"It seems rather a needless risk, if we could do it a better way.... I wonder whether you'd care to trust me with a cheque that I could get a firm I know to put through their account? We could get the money in a couple of days."

"But it could be traced through another bank?"

"I don't know that that would matter. You've got a right to draw cheques on your own account. They wouldn't give you away."

He was slow to answer, and there was reserve in her voice when she spoke again: "But I expect you can think of a better plan. Anyway, you've got the cheque-book now."

He saw that he must have appeared distrustful of the offer, and even ungrateful for what she had already done. He was in danger of losing the one friend he had, at a time when friends were his greatest need. He said: "It isn't that. The fact is I've just been told to clear out before six o'clock. Mr. Rabone knows who I am."

"What did he say?"

He narrated the incident as exactly as possible.

She frowned in thought over this, and then said: "It's bad luck that he's guessed, but I don't think he'll be in any hurry to let the police know. You needn't worry much about that."

He asked with surprise: "You'd advise me to risk it, and stay on."

"I didn't say that. It's not easy to see what's the safest way. But you might leave here and go somewhere that I could reach, if we thought out a plan."

"But you don't think he'll inform the police? You feel sure that he's not that sort?

She answered dryly: "No. He's not that sort."

He attacked the position irritably from another angle: "I suppose he wanted to have you alone here this evening. That's really why he wants me to clear."

She listened to this, and amusement came to her eyes. "I should call that a good guess.... But it isn't that, all the same. Or not that alone. He thinks you've come to the wrong place."

"If you'd only say what you mean!"

"That's what I've been trying to do."

He checked an impatient reply, and made the effort necessary to control a nervous impatience born of the precarious position in which he stood, and remained silent, waiting for her to say more. He was rewarded with: "You told me a good deal. I wonder whether it wouldn't save trouble if I were to pay you back in the same coin."

He became conscious of the boorishness of his previous mood. What obligation had she to him? He said: "Don't tell me anything you're not sure I should know. There's no reason you should. I'd rather trust you than that."

Indeed, if she were not worthy of trust, what hope could he have? He was in her hands, in more ways than one. If she sought to rob or betray him, it would be easy for her to tell a tale that he could not test. In his position, he must trust entirely, or not at all, and his choice was already made.

But she had formed her own resolution, and his words did not change it, but rather confirmed her judgement that she could give a confidence which he would not betray.

"Trust's all right," she said, "but it's simpler to understand. I don't think you'll give me away to Mr. Rabone, and still less that you'll set the police on him, though I shouldn't care if you did, so long as my name wasn't anywhere in the bill....

"Mr. Rabone is a bank inspector. He's on the staff of the London & Northern. Bank inspectors have to be men of good character. If they haven't got private means, the bank expects them to live within their salaries, which are substantial, but nothing more.

"Mr. Rabone is a man against whose financial record nothing is known. He is separated from his wife, but that's understood not to be his fault. She's said to drink like a fish. He has to contribute to her support.

"He lives simply, in such lodgings as these. He takes expensive holidays, but not more so than his salary might cover, particularly if he was careful in earlier years which report says that he was.

"But he gives the impression of having money under control. There was an occasion when he avoided scandal by paying what must have been a large sum, though we haven't been able to find out yet what the figure was.

"No one would have worried themselves to enquire into these matters but for the fact that the London & Northern Bank has been the victim of a succession of forgeries of such a character that there has been a growing suspicion that they could not have been carried out successfully without the assistance, if not the actual direction, of someone with inside knowledge, particularly of the balances lying in the accounts on which the forged cheques were drawn.

"The Texall Enquiry Agency, of which I am one of the humbler members, was instructed, about a year ago, to make the most searching investigation into the records and occupations of about twenty of the bank staff, each of which could have assisted one or other of the robberies at different branches.

"The trouble was that no one man could have been in touch with them all, and when we'd failed to discover anything to connect any of them with the incidents in question, though we'd stirred up some unexpected mud in one or two cases, we received instructions to investigate the private life and connections of some of the higher officials, who had been regarded as above such suspicion before."

"With Mr. Rabone top of the list? Well, I hope you'll prove he's in it up to the neck, as no doubt he is."

Miss Jones smiled. "You don't love him. It's easy to see that. Neither do I.... But we haven't found anything yet, beyond that, if he's really in with a criminal gang, as I think he is, he's an exceptionally circumspect man.

"The only really unpleasant thing that we should be able to prove as yet is that he has a habit of making friends with lonely girls in his lodgings, or when he goes on holidays, and in some other ways, and seducing them without telling them that he has a wife very much alive.

"It was in connection with one of these incidents some years ago that he found it prudent to pay a sufficient sum to a girl, who had a baby coming, to go out to New Zealand with her mother without making a fuss. And when I tell you that, you'll understand why I'm here."

"I should have thought it would have been a better reason for keeping a good distance away."

"Then you didn't listen when I told you what my profession is. I'm a poor girl who's out of a job, and her money down to about ten shillings. I'm rather timid, and more frightened than attracted as yet, but he's very patient and kind, and, in the end, when my money's gone, and—well, what can a poor girl be expected to do...? He's trying hard now to get me a job at the bank, but it's a sure bet that he'll fail in that."

She smiled slightly, and did not change her expression when she saw the lack of response on her hearer's face.

"I wonder," he said, "that you can talk to the filthy beast."

"Oh, I don't know," she said lightly. "Being seduced isn't so bad, when it's being done in a cautious way, and you're playing the timid part."

"And so you've found out nothing yet?"

"Not quite nothing. There have been two dark nights when

he's been visited by callers who come over the roof. The second time, I followed them back. Not closely enough to see who they were, but to find where they went. It was the fourth house from here toward Windsor Terrace. It's quite easy to get along from roof to roof. There's a parapet a foot high, and the dormer windows are close to its inner side."

"It must have been a very dangerous thing to do."

"Oh, I wouldn't say that. It's all in the day's work, or perhaps night's might be a better word.... But if you should see anyone knocking at the front door that you're not anxious to meet, it might be worthwhile trying. I don't know what sort of reception you'd have in the other house, but you might get down before anyone'd try to stop you, and they're not likely to be the sort to call in the police."

"Haven't you found out who they are?"

"Not much yet, but of course we shall. There'll be someone else digging that up now. I have to concentrate here."

"It doesn't sound very circumspect to have criminals crawling over the roofs."

"No? It would be easy to think of other ways more likely to be observed, and not so difficult for us to prove. But I wasn't thinking of that. Most people who make money in criminal ways give themselves away by how they let it slip through their hands. There's not much fun in risking your liberty or your neck for money you never spend, and it's astonishing how little use it is, even if you risk throwing it round. There isn't much that people of bad character can buy, especially in a quiet way, that's much satisfaction to them, and they daren't get drunk for fear of what they might let out.

"But Mr. Rabone lives a quiet frugal life, except for his one annual spree, and this habit I've told you about, which may be the only one he's been able to think of in which he can make his money buy what he wants, without behaving in a way that might come to the bank's ears."

Francis had been sufficiently interested in Miss Jones's narrative to forget, as it had proceeded, the passage of time, and the urgency of his own position; but, as she came to this point, his eyes fell on the clock, and the process of simple mental arithmetic necessitated by Mrs. Benson's explanation of its eccentricity enabled him to see that the question of visiting the bank had answered itself so far as that afternoon was concerned; and this realization brought his mind sharply back to consider how far, if at all, Mr. Rabone's character affected his own precarious security.

"I don't quite see why his being a rotter should make him anxious for me to clear out, even though he may believe that I was one of the Welch lot."

"No?" she said, "but don't you see that if he's in with any criminal gang, the last thing he would wish would be to draw enquiry upon himself, as one who appeared to have been associating with you?

"You know how you walked in through an open door, but the police don't, and they'll do some lively guessing if they find you've been harboured here. There may be more in it even than that. These gangs are often more or less in touch with one another, and we don't know how closely Tony Welch's arrest may have come to some of Mr. Rabone's own associates—that is, of course, if we're right in our suspicions about himself.

"The fact that he knew your assumed name, and recognized you so quickly, makes that rather more likely than not.

"It's easy to see, without bringing me into the picture, that he might prefer you a good distance away; but it doesn't follow that he'd put the police on to you. If we're right as to what he is, it's about the last thing he'd be likely to try."

"Well, the question I've got to decide is whether I'm to clear out as I'm told, or to risk staying another night."

"And you want to get hold of some money first? It's because of that that I've been explaining all this about why I'm here. I wanted you to understand that if you can trust me enough, I really could help you, and in a better way than taking a cheque to the bank counter, though it mightn't be quite so quick. But I might manage even that."

CHAPTER NINE

Half an hour later, Francis sat alone again with his own thoughts. He had small occasion for lively spirits, but he was conscious, beyond reason, of the lightening of heart and hope.

It was not only that he now had a confident expectation of the money that was his most vital need, and that by a method which involved no risk of immediate detection. He was aware that he had found a friend, when his need was greatest, and the probability had been next to none; and though Miss Jones (if such were her real name, which it was easy to doubt) might not be likely to give him the docile companionship and service which had foolishly entered his mind during the earlier day, yet she was likely to be a friend of a better kind than the timid, workless girl he had first thought her to be.

She had now taken a cheque for £20 to her own firm, on the stipulation, willingly agreed, that if the cash resources of the till should not rise to that total, she should bring what she could, and arrange to let him have the balance on a later day.

She had promised to be back before six, and the question of his remaining for a. further night had been left for decision then.

It was evident that, apart from Mr. Rabone's opposition, there could be no more than a precarious safety in a house where his identity was suspected both by his own landlady and a next-door neighbour whose mouth would not be permanently closed. But he was aware that he would go to nothing better than change of perils if he should walk out into the streets to find the shelter of other lodgings where he would be open to the same suspicions, which might become more quickly vocal.

Against that argument, he reminded himself of his resolution to seek proof of his own innocence, toward which he could do nothing while he remained hidden within Mrs. Benson's doors. When he had money at command, he could have little excuse should he delay to use the hours of uncertain liberty to further his one hope of re-establishing himself securely in the respect of his fellowmen.

So reason urged, against a strong reluctance to go. In the few hours that he had known these dingy rooms, they had become hiding-place, and, in a sense, home. But would that feeling have been equally strong if Miss Jones had not been there? Asking himself this, he saw where the greatest source of his hesitation lay. To leave her with that cad—and with the programme to which she had so lightly referred—and not knowing when, nor even if, he would ever see her again—

His mind began to invent a score of reasons why it would be safer to remain until the next morning. He would have more time to look round for such a lodging as he could safely take. He would have time to get much farther away, to some place where suspicion would not be so quickly aroused. He would be able to purchase the luggage which it was so essential to have. To walk in anywhere late at night, and with empty hands, would be to ask for the trouble which he would be almost certain to find!

It was twenty to six when he heard Miss Jones enter, with her own latchkey, at the street-door; and by this time he had arrived at a definite resolution that he would not leave till the next day.

She came in with a smile indicative of the success which she demonstrated next moment by drawing a bundle of notes from her handbag, which she laid on the table, with five shillings in silver.

"By good luck," she said, "there was lots of cash in the till. Mr. Banks made no trouble about changing it. He took my word for it being all right. But he charged five shillings. He's that sort. He won't do anything without being paid."

"I don't mind that."

"No. I didn't suppose you would. Besides, it's a good thing in a way. It makes it a matter of business, and so it's confidential to the firm."

Francis picked up the money. It gave him a sense of freedom and power, to an extent of which he might not have been conscious had he not had those previous penniless hours. He said: "I can't thank you enough. Taking me on trust, in the way you have, and in spite of the things you know—"

"Never mind that," she replied. "There's no time. Mr. Rabone may be in any minute now. The question is, if you're going to leave, how I can get in touch with you again."

"You mean that? It is more than I had a right to ask or expect."

"Well, I thought, if you want to get even with Tony Welch's gang, I might give you some help. We might arrange to meet at the office. There shouldn't be any special risk about that, unless you want to get out of London."

"I don't know that I do.... Anyway, I don't mean to leave here tonight. We'll talk it over tomorrow, when there won't be any pressure of time."

He was pleased to see an expression of satisfaction on her face as he said this. She answered: "I'm glad you've decided to stay the night. I'd been thinking that it might be the safer way. And if we go out together in the morning, the police will be less likely to give you a second look while you've got a companion, and we're talking like friends together.... But if I were you, I should get upstairs before Mr. Rabone comes. It'll save friction, if nothing else. And, if you like, I'll tell Mrs. Benson that I've got some money for you, and I know that you're going to settle with her in the morning."

It was advice which had the tone of a request also, and was of an obvious wisdom. Reluctant though he might be, he had sense enough to go without argument or delay. He would miss the evening meal, but, placed as he was, it would be folly to weigh that against larger issues. He said: "You might tell Mrs. Benson that I'm not very well, and I've gone to bed."

He went upstairs, hearing Mr. Rabone's heavy step in the

hall as he closed his own door.

There was a clothes closet in his room, at the back of which a pile of old books had been pushed away. Among less readable matter, he found a soiled copy of Vanity Fair, with which he tried to divert his mind from wondering what might be going on in the room below.

He listened at times, but there were no sounds that came through his closed door. By the stillness, he might have been the sole occupant of the house.

After a time, he became chilly, and, having no other means of obtaining warmth, got into bed.

He read stubbornly, finding it hard to hold his mind to the words that passed under his eyes. He stopped at times to listen and wonder what might be going on in the room below, at others, his mind wandered to regret the follies of the unchangeable past, or to speculate upon the unpromising future.... And then, unexpectedly, sleep came.

CHAPTER TEN

Francis waked suddenly. He was conscious that he had been sharply disturbed, though he could not tell how. Were the police at the door?

The single electric light was still burning, as it had been when he fell asleep. The book had fallen on to the floor. Was it possible that he had been waked by that?

He listened, and heard nothing. He got up to put out the light. He told himself that it was natural that he should be disturbed by a slight cause, if not none, being the hunted man that he was.

As he got back into bed, he heard light quick footsteps on the floor above. That was in the room which Miss Jones occupied. He had reckoned before this that it must it be over his own. So she was still awake, and up. He heard her door closed and locked. She crossed the floor again with the same quick firm tread. Probably she had just gone up to bed, and it was no more than that which had waked him so thoroughly. It came from going to sleep at so unusually early an hour.

Then what time was it now? He got out again. The only electric switch which the room contained was by the door. He put the light on again, and looked at his watch. The time was 2:17 A.M. A late hour for girls placed in Miss Jones's position to be retiring to bed!

Had she been downstairs with Rabone till now? It was more than nine hours since he had come upstairs as the bank inspector had entered the house. What could she have been doing with him for so endless a time?

But it appeared that whatever might have happened was over now. Certainly, there was nothing that he could do. His interference would be absurd, and would be little likely to be welcomed by her.

Besides, did she not deserve that he should give her a better trust than his doubts implied? Or was that the right word? Jealous he might be, but there was no loyalty that she owed to him.

There were still slight noises over his head. He thought, but was not sure, that he heard her open her window. After that, the sounds ceased entirely. Doubtless, she was in bed. Probably already asleep, as he would be if he had not come up at so confoundedly early an hour....

Horribly through the silence there came the sound of a human scream. It ceased abruptly, as though cut off before it had come to a natural end.

Francis had dozed, but he was widely awake while the sound was still loud on the air. The light in his room still burned. He leapt up. The cry had surely come from the floor above, but not, he thought, from the room over his head.

He had no doubt what he should do now. He must lose no instant to find the cause of that dreadful cry. Yet the tyranny of custom prevailed so far that he delayed to put on some clothes— the circumstances under which he came having left him without a sleeping-suit, so that he had lain down in his shirt—and while he hurriedly half-dressed he heard footsteps, light and quick, crossing the floor over his head, as he had heard them before.

He opened his door to face a house that had become silent again. He switched on a landing-light. He looked down the dark well of the narrow stairs, from which there came no motion, nor light, nor sound. It seemed that the cry, loud and agonized as it was, had been insufficient to disturb Mrs. Benson's rest.

Could there be reason for him to hasten up, where it seemed that nothing was happening now? And what would it be to find?

He looked up, and the silence became sinister. He lost the sense of urgency in that of fear—fear of that which the silence held.

It was the thought of the girl who might be in peril above, or sick with fear in her locked room, that gave him courage to climb the stairs to encounter he knew not what. If, he thought, he had a weapon of any kind. Yet what danger could he expect to meet on the silent landing above?

As he approached it, he became aware of a cold draught, and then had his first surprise on seeing that the bedroom door was open, which he believed that he had heard Miss Jones lock at so late an hour. The opposite door was closed.

He called: "Miss Jones, are you all right?" in a low, and then in a louder voice.

He approached the open door, pushing it wider. The light was switched on. The draught came from the window, which was open. Still getting no reply, he entered the room.

The bed appeared to have been occupied. The clothes had been thrown back, and half on to the floor, as though it had been hurriedly or carelessly left. The room was clearly vacant.

Had she been abducted by criminals who had come over the roofs, perhaps having guessed her to be a detective upon their tracks? Had they murdered her, and dragged her body away? Was it her death-cry that had roused him from sleep?

He did not think that the voice had been hers, but perplexity was mingled with a great fear as he crossed the landing, and knocked upon Mr. Rabone's door.

There was no reply, though he called aloud, and his fear grew. He had no desire to wake the bank inspector without evident cause, and he had most urgent reason for avoiding anything which might involve him in a further publicity, but it had become a matter which he must pursue, at whatever cost.

He tried the handle, and the door opened as it turned. The room was in darkness, and still no one answered his call. Had Rabone also gone in the night?

There was no light on the upper landing. All that entered the room was from the open door opposite. He stepped a pace in, feeling along the wall for the switch which he had missed nearer the jamb, and as he did so he trod on a man's hand, which moved slightly beneath his heel.

He looked down with eyes sharpened by fear, and which were growing used to the gloom. A body sprawled largely over the floor.

He stepped quickly back, and, as he did so, his hand touched the switch which he had avoided before.

The light showed William Rabone lying face downward. If he had any flicker of life, it was yet evident that he was far beyond human aid. His throat was cut, and the dusty carpet was bright with blood.

CHAPTER ELEVEN

Francis stood for some moments, his hand still on the switch. Only his brain moved. He would have had a greater horror of what he saw, had not his heart been cold with the quick instinct of a personal fear.

Should he put out the light, and go back to bed, leaving it for others to discover what it was not his business to know? Who could say that he had been disturbed by a cry which seemed to have aroused no one except himself? But that would be of little avail unless he should have left the house before Mrs. Benson would get about, and perhaps discover that which the attic held. And, if he should slip early away, would it not be like an admission of guilt, especially in the eyes of those who would not, at first, know that he might fly from another fear? Would it not rouse a double urgency of pursuit, before which he would have little chance of escape?

And when he would be caught, it would be necessary to deny everything, to deny that he had ascended the stairs. And if the police, with their systematic, minute investigations, should be able to prove he had, then he would be lost beyond hope!

But by what means could they do that? He looked down on the shoes into which he had thrust his feet without lacing them, in the hurry of his dressing, and he saw that the right one was wet with blood into which he had stepped while the room was dark. There would be enough evidence there to hang anyone who should be fool enough to deny having entered the room, or who should delay to give the alarm.

But why did he assume that it was murder on which he gazed? He had read of men who cut their own throats. But would they give so terrible a cry, if it were an act of deliberate will? It was a question to which he could give no certain reply.

But if it were William Rabone's own act, the weapon with which he had done it could not be far. As to that, it lay near. An open razor. But would a man inflict so wide a wound with his own hand? Again, it was a question to which he could not reply.

A new doubt troubled his mind. It seemed that Miss Jones had fled. Had he died by her hand? Perhaps when she found that the game she played was more difficult than she supposed, and her honour could be secured in no other way? If he should give the alarm, would it be to set pursuit on her track, so that she would not escape, as she might otherwise do? He would curse himself to his last hour, if he should do that, through cowardly fear lest suspicion should fall on him.

Yet was it a probable thing? Was it not more likely that she had been dragged away by the same criminal violence which had left the dead man on the floor? Might it not be urgent that she should be rescued while he stood foolishly there? It was only later that he remembered the light quick step that he had heard crossing the floor *after* the sound of that dreadful cry.

Out of these confused thoughts, a counsel of wisdom came. Was he to accept the character of criminality which had been thrust upon him? But for the experience of the last month, would he not have roused alarm without thought of accusation against himself, as the natural, normal thing for a man to do?

Might it not be his greatest danger that fear should lead him to mimic guilt?

It may have been twenty seconds that he stood motionless with his hand on the switch, while these thoughts went through his mind. Then he turned and went down the stairs, marking each second step with a bloody shoe.

He switched on the lights as he went downward from flight to flight, hesitating a moment as he came to the front passage, with an impulse to open the door on the chance that there might be a policeman whom he could call, but he had an irrational feeling that Mrs. Benson should be first informed of the corpse that her attic held, and he went on to the basement, and knocked loudly on the door where he supposed that she slept.

The woman replied at once, asking what was wrong, in an alarmed voice, to which he answered: "I'm afraid there's something wrong on the top floor, Mrs. Benson. Mr. Rabone's been hurt."

An agitated voice called out: "Mr. Rabone hurt? How could he be hurt...? Well, I'll be coming up. Is he real bad? You'd better go round to Dr. Foster's, if so. He's three doors round the corner in Sefton Street."

As the voice ceased, there were sounds of movement within the room.

Francis stood hesitating. To call a doctor might be a wise thing to do. But he did not like to go out for such a purpose without giving her a more adequate idea of what she would have to face when she should arrive at the top of the attic stairs.

"Yes," he answered, "I'll fetch the doctor at once. But I'm afraid Mr. Rabone's dead. I think he's been killed. I think you ought to let the police know."

He heard a gasping exclamation inside the room. But it seemed that the old woman rose to the emergency, for she called in a firmer voice: "Well, you'd better get the doctor at once. He's the one to say about that. It's no good standing there. I'll get Miss Brown to come in."

She heard her new lodger's feet retire as he obeyed this instruction, and emerged a few moments later hastily dressed, and unbarred the basement door with a shaking hand, to summon Miss Janet Brown.

Francis went out by the front door, which had been chained and bolted as though every burglar in London cast covetous eyes upon Mrs. Benson's ancient furniture. He found Dr. Foster's without difficulty, and a speaking-tube at the side of the night-bell enabled him to inform the doctor of the nature of the case which required his attention.

Dr. Foster said that he would be down in three minutes. What, more exactly, was the address? Francis could not give a number that he now realized that he did not know. He thought (with a moment's discomfort of doubt) that he could find Mrs. Benson's house again without hesitation. It was less easy to describe it to another, and Dr. Foster was decided in mind that he would not risk having to knock up the wrong houses to enquire for a murdered man who was not there. He said that Francis had better wait, and guide him to the address. So he agreed to do, and stood in the street while the three minutes became ten.

Meanwhile, Miss Brown had taken charge of affairs on the scene of the fatality, whether murder or suicide, on which question she expressed her uncertainty in so decided a voice that it had the sound of a final verdict.

She had ascended the top flight of stairs, while Mrs. Benson stood in agitation below, gazed grimly for a long moment at the dead man (whom she had always disliked), and decided reasonably that it was an event of which the police should be informed without further delay.

She returned to her own house, where a telephone was installed, and rang up the police-station.

It happened that Chief-Inspector Combridge had come in, having been detained late in connection with a raid on a gambling den, which had failed through treachery (as he must suppose) among his own staff. He was ill-tempered, and very tired, and on the point of going home, when Miss Brown's tale came over the wire. He said: "Only half a mile away? Have a car round at once. I'll take Potter and Sears."

He got to the house before Francis returned with Dr. Foster. He looked at the dead man, and had no difficulty in deciding that there was nothing a doctor could do which would be useful to him. But he learned that a young lodger, Mr. Edwards, had gone out to fetch one, and admitted it to be an orthodox course of action. He reserved his opinion about Mr. Edwards, as he did about everything. The great need in homicidal investigations is to approach everything with an open mind. At present, the case looked like a prosaic suicide, the cause for which would probably be plain enough when the dead man's circumstances were disclosed. A bank inspector? Ten to one there would be something wrong at the bank. Possibly the man had had warning that investigation was taking place, and had chosen the surest road of escape.... But he would assume nothing. Here was the doctor who had been summoned. It appeared that the lodger was leading him up the stairs.

Inspector Combridge would have preferred that the police surgeon (for whom he had already sent) should have been first on the scene, but he allowed nothing of this to appear in the cordiality of his reception of a medical gentleman who had been properly called in.

His glance passed on quickly from him to the lodger who was showing a modest inclination to retire, of which Inspector Combridge instinctively disapproved. He looked at Francis, who looked at him, and the recognition was mutual.

"So," he said, "this is where you've been hiding, is it? And what am I to think you've been up to now...? You'd better finish dressing, and come back with me. Potter, you can take him in charge."

Francis became conscious for the first time that he had gone out to summon the doctor without vest or coat.

CHAPTER TWELVE

Chief-Inspector Combridge took a few hours of much-needed sleep, and waked to consideration of the problem the night had brought. He was unsure as yet whether he had to deal with a prosaic suicide or a perplexing crime. At present, he had not even ascertained the essential point of whether Rabone had been a left-handed man.

He had learnt the danger of developing theory in advance of facts, and he was not disposed to assume that Harold Vaughan was guilty of murder, because he had been convicted on a quite different charge. But he knew how frequently enquiry concerning those upon whom suspicion falls will disclose a record of previous intimacy with the law. In the case of Vaughan, he admitted in an honest mind that he was less satisfied of his guilt than the jury's verdict had shown them to be. But it was a sinister fact that his antecedents had not been traced, and if he had twice become involved in crimes in which he was not concerned, he was a most unfortunate young man.

Anyway, it was satisfactory to feel that he was securely held. He would be available for questioning, and could be charged at leisure if the evidence should appear to point in his direction.... Satisfactory, also, that his days of defiant freedom had been cut short, and the reproach of being unable to find him had been lifted from the shoulders of the very capable body to which Inspector Combridge belonged. But it was possible to wish that he had been found in a different way. The murder (or suicide) would acquire an additional dramatic interest in the public mind because it had been occasion for the arrest of Vaughan. He saw that, if murder it were, it would be one of those cases in which the prestige of the Metropolitan Police would be too deeply involved to allow failure to be considered. His own reputation also. He was not one to waste many hours in sleep when such a case was waiting investigation....

He interviewed Miss Brown, from whom he heard much, but learned little of value which he did not already know.

He interviewed Mrs. Benson, from whom he learnt more, including certain facts, such as that of Miss Jones's disappearance, which deepened mystery, and others which seemed to increase the probability that Vaughan, possibly in conjunction with the missing girl, was responsible for a brutal crime.

He learnt from Sir Lionel Tipshift's report that suicide was an improbable explanation—might, indeed, be put out of mind, except as a line of defence which they must be prepared to meet when the murderer should be wriggling to dodge the doom that his guilt deserved.

He circulated a description of the missing girl.

He interviewed Sir Reginald Crowe, the chairman of the London & Northern, with whom he had had previous associations, and whom he knew to be his good friend.

Sir Reginald had no charge to make against the dead man. He was reticent on that point. Inspector Combridge could see him again in a few days, when he would be more fully informed, and would give a final reply. Meanwhile, it must be understood that he made no suggestion of any kind: no accusation at all.

He gave the Inspector authority to enquire at the branch where Rabone had kept his own private account, though he understood that it had no abnormal features, and was unlikely to contain anything to assist enquiry. Inspector Combridge, having a different hope, went on to interview the branch manager, and came away well content.

All this was done before 4 P.M., and at this point the Inspector felt that he had come to something too closely resembling a blank wall for his liking—unless the murder could be fixed upon the man who was already under arrest.

He had a case against him, but it was of conjecture and suspicion rather than proof. It was one which a clever counsel might tear to rags. Unless he could find the girl—unless he could be sure what that open window meant—well, he had still to interview Vaughan, and there was hope there. He had deliberately deferred doing this until he had collected all the data that other sources supplied.

Now he would listen with a fair and quite open mind to whatever Vaughan could say in his own defence. It was no evidence that he sought anything but the truth if he anticipated with the confidence of experience that he would obtain a statement which would put the man who would be persuaded to make it in a more precarious position than that in which he already stood.

Even if he were innocent, there would almost certainly be some circumstance which he would desire to conceal, something which might appear to draw suspicion toward himself, which would tempt him to the more dangerous lie. If he were guilty, it would be still more probable that he would make assertions which careful enquiry would overset.

CHAPTER THIRTEEN

The interval which Inspector Combridge allowed to elapse before questioning his recovered prisoner had given Francis an ample leisure in which to consider his own position.

His first bitterness against the malice of circumstance had been blended with an undercurrent of fear, and he was disposed to curse the occasion which had given him such improbable freedom, only to return him to bondage with the threat of a second accusation, and the fear of a far more terrible sentence than that which was already his.

But further thought brought better hope, and the sanguine spirit of youth rose to a vague anticipation that demonstration of his innocence of this greater crime might open the way for reconsideration of the offence of which he was already convicted.

His money, and the cheque-book with its blank counter-foil, were now in the possession of the police, and it was a reasonable conclusion that his identity would be quickly discovered.

Seeing that that which he had suffered so stubbornly to prevent had passed beyond his control, he found an unexpected relief in the thought that he would now be able to acknowledge his identity and could establish contact with his own friends.

He learnt during the day, and felt it to be a good omen, that he was not to be charged immediately with the jail-breaking "offence" he had committed (the law holding, with lamentable absence of humour, that it is the duty of all convicts, even though their cells should be left unlocked, to continue to occupy them for the terms of the sentences they have received), nor was he to be consigned at once to one of the major jails, as would have been the usual routine. If he should not be suspect himself, he saw that he might be reserved as witness of the crime, the perpetrators of which might, for all he knew, be already known to the police, if not actually in their hands.

He was not surprised, nor unwilling, when, at about 5 P.M., he was summoned to leave his cell, and conducted to a room in which Inspector Combridge sat at a broad desk, and some other police officials, whom he did not know, were scattered about.

Inspector Combridge said: "Sit down, Vaughan." His tone was curt, but not unkindly. His hand motioned to a chair opposite his own desk.

As Francis took it, he noticed a police-sergeant at an adjoining table who sat with pen and paper ready to assist the enquiry.

"Two days ago," the Inspector began, "after conviction and sentence, you escaped from custody?"

"I walked out. If he got the chance, I suppose anyone would."

Inspector Combridge did not discuss that. He was merely beginning the examination in an ordinary manner. He asked: "Where did you go?"

"Where you found me."

"Straight there?"

"Yes. The door was open, and I walked in."

"You expected to find it open?"

"No. How should I? I hadn't expected to get away."

"But you might have hoped for acquittal. Where would you have gone then?"

"I hadn't thought about that."

"No? How long had you known Mr. Rabone?"

"I never knew him at all."

"And the young woman—Miss Jones—how long had you known her?"

"I had never met her before."

"Well, we shall see." His voice took a serious tone as he went on: "I want you to appreciate the position in which you stand. You escape from custody. Within two days a man is murdered in a house which otherwise is occupied, so far as we are at present informed, only by two women and yourself. One of the women has disappeared and the other is not under suspicion. You slept on the floor below the room of the murdered man. It appears that you were first on the scene of the crime.

"There is at present no charge against you, and I am under no necessity of warning you, but I tell you now that you are under no obligation to say anything if you prefer to remain silent. In that event, we must establish the truth in our own ways.

"But, if you are innocent of this murder, you may find the truth to be the simplest and wisest in your own interest.

"The fact that you were the first one to raise the alarm obviously is not in itself evidence of any criminal responsibility. But there is one other matter which I must invite you to explain, if you are able to do so.

"You must have been penniless when you entered Mrs. Benson's house. It appears that you made promises of payment to her which you did not keep. The young woman who has disappeared had also been frank in informing her landlady that she was out of work, and that her money was almost gone.

"Last evening, if Mrs. Benson's testimony is to be believed, you retired to your room at a very early hour, possibly to avoid meeting the man who was to be murdered during the night; possibly because you were not in a position to make the payment to Mrs. Benson which you had promised earlier in the day.

"But Miss Jones subsequently gave an assurance on your behalf that you would be able to pay when you came down in the morning.

"At some time between 2 and 3 A.M., Mr. Rabone, who had a habit of carrying a considerable sum in his pocket-book, was murdered, and robbed.

"You were then arrested on the scene of the crime, and you had a sum of over twenty pounds in your pockets."

Francis heard this statement of the case which he had to meet with an outward calmness, for he was conscious that the Inspector watched him keenly for any sign of confusion or admission of guilt. But his heart sank somewhat, for it was a line of attack which he had not expected to hear. In fact, the idea that William Rabone might have been robbed had not previously entered his mind.

But he recognized the fairness with which he was being treated. He was told what the position was, as against himself, and he could be silent or speak at his own choice.

He said: "I didn't have the money from him."

"From Miss Jones?"

"No. Not from her."

"Then will you explain how it came to your hands?"

"I would rather not. I don't really see why I should."

"It is for you to decide. But I will be more frank with you than you are with us. Treasury notes cannot usually be traced. You may be relying on that. But there are exceptions.

"When notes are issued for the first time, there may be records of the numbers of the series which are paid out from the Bank of England, and which are distributed over the counter by the bank which receives them in bulk.

"There were notes of such a kind that Mr. Rabone drew to refill his pocket-book three days ago."

Francis listened to this statement and was not greatly impressed. Actually, the two ten-shilling notes that he had received from William Rabone did not come to his mind.

"I should think," he said, "that that should be very useful to you in discovering the thief."

Inspector Combridge looked his surprise, which he rarely would.

"And that," he asked, "is all that you have to say?"

"Yes. About that. I think it is."

"You still decline to give any explanation of how that money came into your hands during the night?"

"It wasn't during the night."

"Or the day before?"

"Yes. It was my own money. I don't see why I should."

The Inspector's voice was colder than before as he asked:

"Is there any statement that you wish to make concerning the events of the night?"

"Only that I was waked up by hearing a scream, and got some clothes on as quickly as I could, and went up, and found Mr. Rabone dead."

"And Miss Jones? Did you see anything of her?"

"I haven't seen her since I went upstairs about six o'clock."

"You don't know whether she was in her room when you went up?"

"I know she wasn't. Her door was open, and I looked in there first."

"But you don't know whether she was there at the time of the murder?"

"No, how could I?"

"I asked you."

Francis became silent. He remembered the steps he had heard after the scream. He could not say they were hers, though he had little doubt. For all he knew, an admission might be fatal to her. Equally possibly, a lie now might make it vain to help with the truth at a later time, if that should be what her safety required.

He said: "I think I've told you about all I know. But if you're not satisfied, I think I ought to have legal advice before I say more."

Inspector Combridge became silent. The request was one which could not be refused, nor did it occur to him to make any difficulty about it, though it was the technique of these enquiries to get suspected persons to talk, and if possible to sign statements which had been worded for them, before they could have the protection of legal caution.

But his doubt was on different grounds. He had a long experience of such crimes, and of the sometimes very unexpected people by whom they are committed, and he had an instinctive feeling that he must look elsewhere for the hand which had used the razor. He was aware of a number of minor evidences which were consistent with, if they did not actually support, the account which Francis gave of how he had discovered the murdered man.

He saw also that he had as yet no material from which a complete, conclusive case could be built up. In particular, the motive and manner of Miss Jones's disappearance must be resolved.

On the other hand, here was a man with a criminal record, penniless, and in desperate need of the money which had been in the bank inspector's pocket-book. There was motive, opportunity, and the absence of anyone else in the house upon whom suspicion would naturally fall, if he excepted Miss Jones, and Sir Lionel Tipshift was definite in his opinion that it had not been a woman's work. He spoke of a rather tall man, which was slightly in Francis's favour, for he was not of more than medium height. But it was, at least, far more probable that the blow had been struck by him than by a girl of Miss Jones's description, as that had been given to him.

In addition to these arguments of motive and opportunity, and of the absence of any other whom it would be equally natural to suspect, there was the fact that a substantial sum of money had been found upon him, together with a cheque-book, concerning which there had not yet been time for enquiry to be made, but which would, in all probability, be found to have come from the possession of the murdered man.

He knew that two of the notes certainly had, and it would require a very good explanation to induce any jury to believe that their transit had been of an innocent kind, or that the remainder of the money had not been taken from the same source.

Now, an invitation for such explanation was met by refusal, followed by request for legal assistance. That, if there were no innocent explanation to give, was precisely what Inspector Combridge's experience would expect to hear. He saw that it gave him reasonable ground for charging Harold Vaughan with complicity in the crime, which he might otherwise have delayed to do.

He said: "As you do not offer any explanation of how the money came into your possession, it becomes my duty to charge you with the murder of William Rabone, and I have to warn you that anything you say may be used in evidence against you."

"I have nothing to say, except that I have told you the truth already, I had nothing to do with the murder, and don't know who did it."

"Very well. What solicitor would you like to have?"

Francis thought of the firm who had undertaken his defence previously, on Tony Welch's instructions. In the result, he was landed here. That might not be their fault, but they were men whom he did not like. He had known, while they had been active and cunning in his defence, that they had assumed his guilt. No doubt, most of their clients were justly charged.

He thought of Mr. Jellipot, who had been his father's solicitor, and to whom, in his own person, he would most naturally go. Well, he supposed, in any event, his identity must be revealed now. He had a vague idea that Mr. Jellipot was not a criminal lawyer, but he felt that to be an advantage rather than otherwise. The austere respectability of that conveyancing office seemed to thrust the ideas of confidency-trickery or brutal murder further away, as though it should be sufficient for Mr. Jellipot to appear in court saying: "There is some mistake: this is Mr. Hammerton, a client of mine," and he would be released, with respectful apologies, from the dock.

After a moment's hesitation he mentioned Mr. Jellipot's name.

CHAPTER FOURTEEN

Being returned to his cell without further questioning, Francis had the benefit of ample leisure in which to consider the position to which he had fallen.

It is an unpleasant experience to be charged with murder, which a consciousness of innocence may not greatly relieve, if it be difficult to demonstrate it to other minds. And though he might still have a fairly confident hope that the truth would be discovered in time to relieve him from any capital peril, he saw that he had done something to draw needless suspicion upon himself by his lack of frankness concerning the assistance he had received from Miss Jones during the previous day; only realizing how much it might be when he recollected those two ten-shilling notes which had come from Mr. Rabone's pocket-book, and the numbers of which, he could have little doubt, had been traced, with the presumption following that he had obtained the whole sum from the same source.

Still, that could be, more or less, rebutted by the evidence of the cashed cheque, which must surely be traced, whether he would or no, through the cheque-book which was now in possession of the police.

Had it been foolish not to be frank in immediate explanation? He saw that he had acted on an instinctive impulse rather than any reasoned calculation—an impulse prompted by vague fear that he might involve the girl in some trouble which he could not estimate while he remained ignorant of what had actually happened on the attic floor; of which, as far as his knowledge went, she and Rabone had been the only occupants.

Did he therefore judge her himself as being guilty of that brutal murder? Surely that went beyond a logical deduction from what he did. His own position showed that innocence was no safeguard against suspicion and even conviction of serious crime.

But, in fact, what did he know of her? An acquaintance of a few hours. One who had told him a tale which might be fiction from end to end; or, more probably, compounded of false and true, as expediency or fear might have prompted her to invent or withhold in the precarious confidence she gave to a stranger who was himself under something more than suspicion of criminality.... Well, he supposed that Mr. Jellipot would be here soon, and he could resign his difficulties to the solution of that cautious, judicial mind

But it was while he reflected thus that a warder entered his cell bringing an enquiry from the Inspector. Had he another lawyer whom he would like to call, or should they communicate with Moss & Middleton, who had defended him at his previous trial? It appeared that Mr. Jellipot had declined to come.

Francis would have been more dismayed at this information had not incredulity dominated his mind.

"Why," he said, "he'd never do that! He's been our lawyer from my grandfather's." And then he perceived the trap in which he was caught. What did Mr. Jellipot know of Harold Vaughan?

Was it consonant to the dignity of that quiet and elderly lawyer to undertake the defence of a convicted confidence-trickster who had broken jail, and was now accused of robbery, and a most sordid and brutal murder? Probably he had been resentful of the effrontery which had dared to misuse his name!

Actually, Mr. Jellipot's reaction to the unexpected call had been somewhat different. He had been mildly surprised; and puzzled as to how the accused man should have been led to call upon him.

He had had little practice in the criminal law, but, like many others, he had a secret confidence in his ability to excel in that direction in which he was of an untested skill. He had been somewhat flattered, even tempted. But he was no longer young. His practice, always solid and sound, had been greatly increased since he had won the respect and confidence of Sir Reginald Crowe, in connection with earlier events with which this narrative is not concerned, and that energetic banker had rewarded him with a bulk of business which would not otherwise have found its way to his office.

Now he remembered several matters of importance with which tomorrow and the following days should be fully concerned. He looked at the clock, and became aware that it was the time at which he was accustomed to pick up any papers which he wished to study in uninterrupted leisure, and go home to dine at his comfortable flat in Hartington Gardens. He felt a most natural reluctance to start off in an opposite direction at such an hour, to be detained—who could say how long?—in a police-court cell while his dinner spoiled.

He said, with polite firmness, that he did not know the prisoner, and that it was a class of business which he did not usually undertake.

Doubtless, it would have been a final decision, with consequences, bad or good, for several people who were unaware of the trembling of the scales of fate, had not Francis had a fortunate inspiration. He asked for, and received, permission to speak to the solicitor on the telephone himself.

Mr. Jellipot, already rising to leave his office, returned to the telephone, and heard a voice which seemed vaguely familiar, though he could not place it. He heard it pleading with him to grant an interview, however short, before declining the case. It did not sound, to his trained instinct, like that of a vicious and murderous criminal. It was human, personal, more difficult to refuse than the formal police request he had received a few minutes before.

Hesitating, he was lost. He found himself saying that he would be there within half an hour.

CHAPTER FIFTEEN

Jesse Banks was an alert lean man, with a hard keen face, and a reticence, both of speech and expression, which fitted him for success in the peculiar profession that he practised, and judging by the extent of his staff, or the manner of his private life, he had not failed to attain it.

Now Miss Jones sat in his office, and gave an account of her night's adventures. The narrative was long, but he listened without interruption, regarding her the while in an expressionless manner, giving no indication of what he thought. He had no reason to complain of any lack of clarity on the part of one whom he rightly considered to be of exceptional ability for such investigations, and of a character not often united with the special qualifications which her occupation required.

She concluded: "I don't suppose I could prevent the police finding me sooner or later, even if it were wise to attempt, but I thought you ought to have my report first. So I went straight home, and stayed there till I was sure that they were not on my track.... But I suppose they'll trace that cheque here, sooner or later, even if they don't find cause to look in this direction about anything else."

It was midday when this conversation took place, and, knowing the office routine, she had no doubt that the betraying document would have been deposited in the London & Northern Bank about two hours earlier.

But it appeared that the usual routine had not been followed. The cheque was still in the safe.

"They won't trace you through that. Not yet," Mr. Banks said. "But it must be paid in at once." He touched a bell to give the necessary instructions. He answered her puzzled silence with more explanation than he would often give: "Because it's the obvious thing to do."

She saw that his first thought had been that he did not intend that his own office should appear to be implicated in irregularity of any kind.

He added: "You've done quite rightly. I've no doubt the whole thing will have to come out. You've got nothing to fear. But our instructions are from Sir Reginald Crowe, and it's to him that we must report. We'll have some lunch first, Miss Weston, and then go on to the bank."

He rose with the word, and led the way out, only pausing to give instructions that Sir Reginald's secretary should be rung up at the head office of the London & Northern, to say that he would be calling upon him at 2:45 P.M., on a matter of urgency.

The time was the earliest at which the banker could be expected back from his own lunch, and gave them ample time for a leisurely meal.

Mary Weston had no cause to complain of the fare which her employer provided, or of any lack of courtesy on his part, but, under more normal circumstances, she might reasonably have called the meal dull.

He was evidently occupied upon the problem of Mr. Rabone's death, and his conversation was confined to an occasional question, with long intervals of silence, which she had too much discretion to interrupt.

He asked once: "You couldn't give any clue to the man who went over the roof? No idea what he looked like at all?"

"No. I told you that. Not the least. He had a good start, and I didn't catch him up. Indeed, as he went on, he got farther away. I expect he knew the roof better than I did; and I had to look where I was going, rather than try to see him. Anyway, it would have been too dark."

She added: "I got nearest to him when he was getting in at

the window. He was some time doing that. I suppose he was anxious not to make any noise. But even then I had to keep far enough away for him not to know I was there."

"So you would. And it was a dark night. If you didn't see, it's no use saying you did. Should you say he was a tall man?"

"Honestly, I couldn't say in the least."

"Pity. But I don't see how anyone could expect you would."

After an interval of silence, he asked again: "You feel sure Rabone suspected you?"

"I know he did last night. He didn't suspect: he knew. He may have done all along. I can't say about that."

"Perhaps so. But it doesn't seem likely." He added, after an interval, less to her than as one speaking aloud: "At present, it looks more like suicide than anything else—suicide as the result of something he'd just heard—but we shall have Tipshift's opinion on that point."

He called for his bill, and took a taxi to the head office of the London & Northern Bank.

CHAPTER SIXTEEN

Francis Hammerton, standing the following morning in the dock of the Magistrates' Court, heard himself charged, in the name of Harold Vaughan, with the wilful murder of William Rabone, together with some further offences of subordinate but sufficiently serious character.

He heard Inspector Combridge give formal evidence of his arrest, after which Mr. Dunkover, who had been briefed for the Crown, rose and said that he did not propose to call further evidence. He asked for a week's remand.

The magistrate, Mr. Garrison, looked at the solicitor to the accused: "Any objection, Mr. Jellipot?"

Mr. Jellipot replied in a hesitant manner. He lacked the carrying voice and the confident demeanour of the advocate who is accustomed to practise in the criminal courts. Mr. Garrison, who had occupied his seat of office for twenty years with an ever-increasing reputation, both for good law and good sense, and for an occasional witticism which might even be considered worthy of repetition by the American press, had a moment's doubt as to whether the prisoner could be considered fortunate in the solicitor he had instructed.

"It is an application," Mr. Jellipot said, with a slow formality, and in the tone of one who advises a client on an intricate point of law, "which I cannot resist. But I must ask you to allow me to express the reluctance with which I agree, my client being anxious to meet and repudiate the charge which has been made against him at the first possible moment."

Mr. Garrison, looking keenly at the speaker, was inclined to a revision of his first opinion. He decided that Mr. Jellipot might be more sheep-like than leonine in his aspect, but that he was a sheep who might stand his ground in a very obstinate way. The manner might be diffident, but there was a fighting quality in the words which did not suggest that there would be any lack of confidence in the way in which the prisoner's defence would be set up.

"Very well," he said. "Ten A.M. on the thirteenth. That convenient?"

He glanced at Mr. Dunkover, who half rose, and bowed. Francis felt a warder's hand on his arm. He was hurried from the dock to make way for a costermonger whose barrow was alleged to have obstructed the Park Lane traffic....

An hour later, Inspector Combridge was received by Sir Reginald Crowe in his private office.

"I've got some rather interesting information for you," the banker said, "but before we go into that I think I ought to tell you that I've just had Jellipot on the phone, and I've asked him to come here as quickly as he can.... The fact is that he says he's sure you've got the wrong man."

If Inspector Combridge felt any pleasure in hearing this, he concealed it successfully. He knew Mr. Jellipot, with whom he had been associated previously in a very difficult and dangerous case. He liked him personally, and respected his abilities. But that did not alter the fact that they were now on opposite sides, and he was not one who would allow personal friendships to impede his duty, or deflect his judgement. He knew that Sir Reginald was always more likely than not to take the unusual course; but, to his mind, the fact that he was personally acquainted with the accused's lawyer was a particular reason why they should not meet to discuss the case in unofficial ways.

He replied cautiously: "Well, of course, he's got to say that."

"So he has. But in this case you can take it from me that it's what he really believes. I may say he's sure. Anyhow, he's willing to give you some facts that you wouldn't be likely to get so easily or completely in other ways."

"Of course, I'll listen.... I know you wouldn't lead me up the wrong path.... He'll have to say what he thinks wise at his own risk.... We've found out a few things ourselves."

"Traced Miss Jones?"

"Not yet. But we soon shall. It seems probable that she was one of the gang, even if she didn't have any part in the actual crime. From her description, it's practically certain that it was she who got the cheque-book from the bank that we found in Vaughan's pocket. She used a note that's certainly forged, though we haven't had time to follow that up yet. I've sent a man to interview a Mr. Hammerton, in whose name it was obtained, and I shall know more about that before the day's over."

Sir Reginald looked amused. He controlled an expression the Inspector did not enjoy, to ask: "You think that Vaughan and the girl were both members of a forging gang?"

"That's how it looks. We know something about Vaughan's character and associates from the conviction we've obtained against him already. We don't know anything about the girl yet, except this cheque-book business, and the way she escaped.... By the way, there was one cheque gone from the book. If it's been used, we may get some help from that."

Sir Reginald smiled openly. "I think you'll find that it has.... You say you know how the girl escaped, if that's the right word to use?"

Inspector Combridge, being very far from a fool, saw that Sir Reginald must know more of these matters than he had yet said; but he suppressed a slight and not unnatural feeling of annoyance. It was his business to get at the truth, from whatever source, and whatever it might prove to be. He did not doubt that the banker would give him all the help he could, in his own way. But he was human enough to wish to show that he had his own sources of information, and that he had already learnt some things of which Sir Reginald might not be aware.

"Yes," he answered. "We know how she got away, or, at least, we're practically sure; and it's that that seems to show what she really is.

"There's a house nearby—four doors away—where there's a lodger in whom we've been interested for a long time past, and by scratches on the roof and windows, and other signs, it's evident that people have been in and out between the two places, probably more than once.

"You'll probably find, before we've finished, that that's why Rabone chose to lodge in an attic room.... But you'll see that, if the girl knew the way to escape to that house, it's a black mark against her."

"Have you any proof that she did?"

"There's the open window in her room, and the fact that she must have gone by the roof, because there was no other way. And—beyond that—there's another lodger—not the man we're after—one on a lower floor—who heard footsteps going down the stairs during the night that sounded to him too light for those of a man."

"I can see you haven't been losing time.... Inspector, we're going to help each other quite a lot in this matter.

"...I've got a witness for you myself, a Miss Weston, with a tale you'll be quite interested to hear.... But Jellipot may be at the door any moment now, and before he comes I've got something to show you that bears on the crime—if such it were—from another angle."

Sir Reginald took a letter from his desk, and passed it over to the Inspector.

"That," he said, "appears to have been written by Rabone less than two days ago. It was received by our General Manager yesterday. It isn't conclusive, of course. But read in the light of the investigation we were making, and of his death or suicide a few hours after it was written—"

"It wasn't suicide. That's certain."

"Very well. Murder."

The Inspector's attention was already concentrated upon the letter. He read:

DEAR SIR,

In reference to the recent forgeries which have caused, and are still causing, so much loss to the Bank, I should be obliged if you would grant me a private interview, at which I could place certain facts before you.

Yours faithfully,

WILLIAM RABONE

Inspector Combridge considered this document carefully.

"As it reads," he asked, "might it not be the letter of an honest man, who had made certain discoveries in the course of his work, by which his suspicions had been aroused?"

"Yes, on the face of it, so it might. No doubt, that is intended to read. But he would hardly have asked for a private interview with the General Manager under such circumstances. He would have included it in his ordinary report, or perhaps communicated direct with the Committee which has this investigation in hand. Or, had it been a case of urgency, he would not have proceeded by letter at all. He would have come here at once."

Before the Inspector could discuss these aspects of the matter, Mr. Jellipot was announced.

CHAPTER SEVENTEEN

Mr. Jellipot shook hands with a quiet cordiality. He felt confident both in the strength of his own case and in the goodwill of those to whom he proposed to state it. He observed, without resentment, the slight official constraint in the Inspector's manner which it must be his part to dispel.

He said: "I'm glad you've brought us together, Sir Reginald. It seems to me that this is a case where we've got to pool all that we know, if the guilt is to be laid at the right door. And so long as we're all wasting our wits over the question of Francis Hammerton's complicity in a crime with which he had nothing to do, beyond—"

"Who did you say?" the Inspector asked sharply. He remembered the name in which the cheque had been drawn.

"I said Francis Hammerton. That's my client's true name, as he ought to have had the sense to tell you before."

The Inspector was quick to see the implications of the new fact. He said: "Then the order for the cheque-book which his accomplice secured was signed in his true name?"

"Naturally so. But I don't know that you should describe the young lady in that way. If," he smiled, "I am correctly instructed, she may turn out to be Sir Reginald's accomplice rather than his. But," he added cautiously, "I am not acting for her, nor am I directly concerned for the veracity of the explanation which she appears to have given of her acquaintance with Rabone."

Inspector Combridge, while still warily conscious that he must not allow either friendship or respect for Mr. Jellipot to warp his official judgement, was sufficiently well acquainted with him to know that he would not be likely to speak as he did without a solid basis of fact to support his words. He saw also that there was information to be gained, probably from both of his present companions, beyond anything he could have anticipated a few moments before, and which it might be vital for him to have. But even now he did not overlook the importance of maintaining an independent position.

"If you think," he said, "it to be to your client's interest to disclose the line of defence which he intends to set up, of course I shall be glad to listen."

"His defence is that he discovered the murder exactly as he told you when he was first asked. Beyond that, I propose to show that he is an absolutely respectable young man, who was foolish enough to make some undesirable friends, and lacked the moral courage to give his true name when he found himself in a particularly distasteful mess."

The Inspector considered this. He observed a possibility—no more—that it might be true; but even if that might be, it seemed a good deal to attempt to demonstrate in the present position. And there were some awkward facts which might excuse doubt of Vaughan's—or Hammerton's—absolute innocence in a less sceptical mind than that of an inspector of the Metropolitan Police.

"You're putting it rather high," he said. "After all, he's a convicted criminal. I don't see how you get over that."

"There's the Court of Appeal."

The Inspector did not dispute the fact, but was doubtful of its use in the present case. "You know," he said, "they won't listen to fresh evidence, if the accused himself withheld it at the trial. They'll say it's too late for that now."

"It is a difficulty," Mr. Jellipot admitted, "which I have already observed. But I hope that we may find a way through."

The Inspector did not fail to notice that Mr. Jellipot used the plural "we" as though alluding to his present company, and being confident of their co-operation. He said: "Well, of course, if you can convince me of Hammerton's innocence, I'll do all that I can. But you won't find it an easy job. What about his pocket being full of Rabone's money when he was arrested half an hour afterwards?"

"The reply is that it wasn't. It was full of his own. You'll find that the blank counterfoil in the cheque-book is a sufficient explanation of that."

Sir Reginald interposed for the first time. "Yes, Inspector, I think you'll find that he succeeded in cashing the cheque. I've had confirmation of that."

"But two of the notes have been traced to Rabone's possession."

Mr. Jellipot replied by narrating the circumstances under which they had passed into his client's hands.

"It is an explanation," the Inspector said dryly, "which would have been more convincing had he told me at first."

Mr. Jellipot conceded that. "So it would. The fact is he forgot."

The explanation reduced the Inspector to a silent consideration of its plausibility, and in the resulting pause Sir Reginald said: "Gentlemen, I don't know how you feel, but it's about the time when I begin to have a decided inclination for a good lunch.

"I can't let you go yet, because I want you to meet Mr. Banks of the Texall Enquiry Agency, and a Miss Weston—a charming girl—who'll both have some things to tell you that you'll find it worth while to hear.

"I've asked them to come at two o'clock, and as I thought the Inspector mightn't like to be seen lunching publicly with the solicitor on the other side, I've ordered a little meal to be brought in here."

Neither of the gentlemen concerned making any objection to this hospitable arrangement, they lunched together accordingly, Sir Reginald leading the conversation skilfully backward to a time when they had been allied in the pursuit of a common foe, until Mr. Banks and Miss Weston were shown into the room.

CHAPTER EIGHTEEN

It is a commonplace of the fiction of crime that the brilliant amateur will discover elusive murderers whose identity will be hidden from the slower-witted officers of the law. But in this inferiority of truthful narrative it may appear, at this stage at least, that the official mind of Inspector Combridge, and the civilian one of the Head of the Texall Enquiry Agency, were of a close equality, whether of dullness or perspicuity; for it appeared, when they met in Sir Reginald's office, with no excess of cordiality on either side, that they had come to the same decision as to the identity of the wanted man.

In arriving at this conclusion it was already evident that Mr. Banks had had the benefit of the knowledge of some circumstances of the crime of which the Inspector had not been equally well informed, but if we regard the matter with an entire impartiality we must observe also that Mr. Banks had not had the benefit of hearing Sir Lionel Tipshift's opinion that the crime had been the work of a left-handed man.

It was after Miss Weston had completed a narrative which may be conveniently deferred, as it was given with greater precision in the witness-box on a later day, that Mr. Banks said, "Well, I don't know what you think, Inspector, but I should say that you won't have to look farther than the top floor of number seven to find the man that you want."

"Meaning Entwistle?"

"Meaning Long Pete, of course. That's what he's mostly called in his own crowd."

The Inspector was aware of the name usually applied to Peter Entwistle in the criminal circles that were supposed to make use of his skill. But he dissented from the enquiry agent's description.

"His own crowd?" he said. "You can't say there's any to which he really belongs. That's been what's kept him clear of our hands for the last ten years, and he making a fortune the while, at a safe guess. He doesn't drink, he doesn't gamble, he doesn't mix with any of the gangs among whom we may have one or two who know how to give us the information we want at the right time; and so he's kept out of our hands for more years than one of his kind probably ever did since we've been an organized force."

"The gentleman," Sir Reginald interrupted, "seems to be an interesting character. Do you mind telling me what his occupation is supposed to be, and why you conclude that he's the most likely man to have murdered a bank inspector four doors away?"

Inspector Combridge answered: "It's a matter of deduction, of course. I'm not sure that we've got evidence enough even to justify an arrest. But that's been the difficulty with Mr. Entwistle since I heard of him first in connection with the Bradwell forgeries, nearly ten years ago.

"He's a handwriting expert, and an artist in more ways than one. He taught engraving for two years at a Municipal Technical School in North London, and since he gave that up he's been doing landscape painting—actually sold one or two pictures, I believe, for moderate amounts.

"But his main occupation, if he isn't a greatly misjudged man, is that of forging cheques and other documents.

"He does just that, and no more. He won't mix himself up in procuring specimen signatures, or passing the documents, or— in fact, in anything but the actual use of his pen; and it's said that he only asks a ten per cent commission on the face value of the cheques he forges, but he insists on that, cash down at the time, and won't listen to other terms.

"It follows that he only deals with those gangs that are well-established and well-financed, and you can see that if he does nothing to give himself away, he isn't easy to catch.

"We've laid traps for him more than once, but he's been too wary to walk in; and we've tried, without any success, to get someone to give him away.

"The curious thing about him is that he's ambidextrous. He's called left-handed, but that's not exactly correct. He can imitate some signatures with his right hand, and some with his left; and, with one or other, he'll sign your name so that you'll swear it's genuine yourself, though you can't remember writing it.

"He's never made any secret of that capacity—boasts of it, in fact—and of course it's no crime to be expert with a pen; and being so open about it is in his favour rather than not. But we've known what he's done more than once, and only been just short of the legal proof which would have justified an arrest."

"You mean," Sir Reginald replied, "the forging of cheques, such as those which have been causing such losses to us?"

"Yes. It's never been less than an even guess that they were his work, and it's ten to one now."

"But how far does that connect him with Rabone's death?"

"It's only inference, as I've said. But here's a man leaving Rabone's window immediately after he's killed, and Miss Weston follows this man—though she can't say who he was—to the window of the house where Entwistle lives. And there's a man named Bigland on the floor below him, who was wide awake enough to hear her feet going down the stairs, when she escaped by the same way, but didn't hear anyone who would have had a much heavier tread.

"And there's the fact that Rabone had visitors before who came to him over the roof, and from where else would they be? We can't suppose that it was a general habit in that street to make midnight calls on Mr. Rabone over the slates.

"When you add to that the conspiracy that Rabone was either engaged in himself or on the point of discovering—you can read this letter either way, but it's got to be one of the two—and the occupation by which we've no doubt that Entwistle lives, and you've got the kind of case with which we usually have to begin. We know the fact well enough, and we've just got to settle down on it till we've built up the formal proof that the law requires.

"I don't say that we've got it yet, by a long way, especially as there's no legal evidence of motive of a kind that we should be allowed to mention in court; but there's one point that helps a little, and that is that Sir Lionel's almost sure that it was the work of a left-handed man, who attacked Rabone from behind."

"Well," Mr. Banks commented on this somewhat lengthy statement of the official attitude, "if that isn't enough to justify you in laying him by the heels, I must say you're not easy to please."

"Perhaps I'm not. But it seems that we've got to own up to one mistake already, and that's more than enough. We can't risk an acquittal for lack of evidence, on the top of that, or perhaps even a discharge from the Magistrates' Court."

"I thought," Sir Reginald interposed again, "that it was a theory at the Yard that criminals always keep to their own type of offence. Is Mr. Entwistle supposed to be equally addicted to violent murder and forging cheques? The combination's rather unusual, isn't it?"

"Yes," the Inspector admitted frankly, "so we do; and so, no doubt, it is. And if this were a crime committed under rather different circumstances, I should say it would let Entwistle out. If it were a case of violent homicide in the course of a burglary, for instance, we shouldn't give him a thought.

"But you've got to consider the position of a very cautious and successful criminal who's avoided all contact with the law, as very few criminals do, and who (we may suppose) suddenly finds himself in desperate peril because Rabone's going to squeal, and he takes the one course that remains. It's a crime that grows naturally, so to speak, from what he has done before, however different its kind.

"He must be an exceptionally wily and cool-blooded character, or he wouldn't have walked free as long as he has."

"And you think"—Sir Reginald's tone was still doubtful—" that this murder was planned in a way that makes it look consistent with what his character's likely to be? There's not much discretion in changing a risk of being arrested for forgery for a seat in the condemned cell."

"Perhaps not. But he couldn't guess that Miss Weston would be hopping out on to the roof. And as to the condemned cell—well, he's not there yet!"

It was a statement which Sir Reginald could not dispute. But he saw reason to hope that the Inspector's diagnosis of the position was correct; for, if so, he might have a sound expectation that the losses that his bank had suffered during recent years would have reached an end, and that in a way which he much preferred—without the publicity which a prosecution on the direct issue would have involved.

CHAPTER NINETEEN

Mr. Jellipot went back to his office, conscious of some arrears of work which would keep him later than it was his habit to stay, but content that the afternoon had not been wasted. He felt that Inspector Combridge was finally convinced of Francis Hammerton's innocence of the graver charge, though he was modest enough to attribute this result more to Miss Weston's eloquence than his own.

That being so, he had been content to leave the charge hanging over his client's head until the remand hearing in a week's time.

The Inspector had, in fact, never felt satisfied that Francis Hammerton had been more than an accessory in, or perhaps after, the crime; and that suspicion had been based mainly on the possession of the money, which had now been plausibly explained away. His best hope, which he had now put aside, had been that the murder charge would have induced a confession by which it would have become possible to fix the guilt upon the principal criminal.

But Mr. Jellipot had seen that the Inspector was reluctant to go to the length of publicly abandoning the case against Francis Hammerton until he should be prepared to demonstrate the activity of his Department by another arrest. As a more serious argument, he had said that the difficulty of establishing a case against the man whom he now regarded as the almost certain criminal might be increased if it were publicly known that the charge against Harold Vaughan had been withdrawn. At present, the criminal must be easy in the belief that the police were working to build up a case against an absolutely innocent man, and one who could do nothing to give him away, knowing nothing of whom he was, or of the circumstances that had led up to the crime.

Mr. Jellipot, accepting this position, had made a bargain which might be to his client's future advantage, and was certainly conducive to his present peace. He had stipulated that, if he should concur in Francis Hammerton remaining under the charge of murder for another week (which he had no legal means of preventing, though he might have urged arguments to which Inspector Combridge would not have refused to listen), his true name should not be made public at the remand hearing, unless the course of the proceedings should render it a disclosure which could not be avoided.

When he reminded himself that his client was already convicted on another charge, and that the withdrawal of that of murder would make no immediate change in the fact of his confinement, and might even be unfavourable to its conditions, he concluded that the bargain was not one of which Francis could have cause to complain.

He turned his mind to the greater difficulty with which he was still confronted—that of proving his client's innocence of a crime of which he had been already convicted.

CHAPTER TWENTY

During the remainder of the week, two things happened which, though not of spectacular character, were important in their influence upon the events of the drama which was to come.

First of these, Mr. Jellipot drew up and entered an appeal against his client's existing conviction, in which, though it may have exhausted the legal possibilities of the case in the grounds which it set out, he admitted to his own mind that he had a very limited confidence. But, bold in his cautious way, he intended to make a use of it, as soon as his client should be clear of the capital charge, which would not only be to his immediate benefit, but through which he hoped that further evidence might be procured, of such a nature that the Court of Appeal would not refuse to hear it.

Of perhaps equal, though different importance, was the information that came to Inspector Combridge, as he was vainly searching for additional evidence against Mr. Peter Entwistle, sufficient to justify him in applying for a warrant for his arrest, that that gentleman had disappeared.

His first feeling on hearing this was annoyance, and some anger with his subordinates, who had failed in the duty of observation which had been entrusted to them. Yet he had satisfaction in observing the implications of this disappearance. He knew that actually, if not legally, it is very near to an admission of guilt for a man to take flight under such circumstances, before the hunt has been opened upon him.

He decided that Entwistle, possibly having received a hint

that the case against Harold Vaughan was not satisfactory to the police, had decided that it would be prudent to go into some hiding-place—perhaps already prepared against such an emergency—until the result of the present prosecution should appear. Should Harold Vaughan be convicted, or even should his trial conclude without indication that suspicion might be pointing in his own direction, he might then return to his former haunts with his usual coolness, or perhaps decide that it had become time to retire in comfort, to enjoy the fruits of his ten years of successful crime.

And so, by his own action, he had both supplied the Inspector with an additional reason for applying for a warrant against him, and increased his confidence that in so doing he would not be arresting the wrong man a second time.

He talked the matter over with Mr. Jesse Banks, with whom he was careful to keep in contact, recognizing, among other reasons, that that gentleman's investigations on behalf of the London & Northern ran closely alongside those on which he was more immediately engaged, and, being supported by his almost equally experienced opinion, he took out a warrant.

Fortified with this document, he searched Mr. Entwistle's two attic rooms, and was more annoyed than surprised to find that, though they had been abruptly left, they contained no incriminating evidence of any kind.

He did not anticipate any prolonged delay in effecting the arrest of the missing man, knowing that it is almost impossibly difficult for any man to remain concealed from his fellows, even with the assistance of the resources which he supposed Peter Entwistle to possess, when the interests of press and public have been united in his pursuit. And he reflected with satisfaction that a figure of unusual height and leanness is not easily overlooked or disguised.

For three days the search was conducted throughout the country with the routine efficiency of the police, but without enlisting the aid of the press, or taking other steps to make Peter Entwistle's disappearance publicly known.

On the fourth morning, the Inspector, happening to meet Mr. Banks, admitted to him that the arrest had not yet been made. When he added that he had decided that the time had come when he must appeal to press and public to assist the search, the enquiry agent answered doubtfully: "Yes? You should know best about that. But it's the eleventh now, and I should say he'll be in court on the thirteenth, if he isn't scared before then. Might be worth waiting to see."

Inspector Combridge said that he would think it over, and having done so he decided that it was a hint worth taking. He knew the tendency that most criminals have to attend trials in which they are actually or potentially interested, and he saw that if Entwistle thought that his disappearance had not been remarked, and had probably therefore been a result of unfounded fear, he would be more likely to venture into Mr. Garrison's court than if he were advertised over England as a wanted man.

Anyway, it was no more than two days to wait. The ports were watched. He had ascertained that, if Entwistle had a passport at all, which was improbable, it had not been taken out in his own name. He resolved to wait.

CHAPTER TWENTY-ONE

Francis Hammerton had by this time acquired a sufficient experience of the routines of the criminal courts to feel that the dock was a quite natural position in which to stand.

He entered it on this occasion with the comforting assurance that the charges of murder and larceny were to be withdrawn, and with the further knowledge that Mr. Jellipot was moving either for a new trial, or for the quashing of his previous conviction.

Yet such is the perversity of human nature that he was conscious of a more clamant misery than when he had stood there a week before, and heard himself preposterously charged with the murder of a man whom he scarcely knew, and against whom he had no cause of quarrel. He had known then that, even if he were relieved of that monstrous suspicion, which his mind declined to accept as more than a passing cloud, he was yet hopelessly condemned to a long term of confinement, with all the calculated degradations that the modern prison inflicts, and with the ultimate difficulty of resuming the life from which he would so strangely have disappeared.

He had been desperate before, but he was now tortured with doubtful hope; for Mr. Jellipot, conscious of the legal difficulties with which he was confronted, and anxious not to raise too confident anticipation in his client's mind, had been so cautious in forecasting the results of the application that he was about to make, that he had done no more than raise a hope so faint as to be more torturing than despair.

He saw no one he knew. He met Mr. Garrison's eyes, keenly and yet distantly regarding him. He saw the row of legal gentlemen who had combined in disposing of his case so expeditiously the week before. He saw the uniformed policemen about the doors, and the motley crowd of spectators, who would have been more numerous had there not been a report circulated that the police would ask for a further remand, and that, on this occasion, there would be little to hear or see.

He saw Miss Jones in one of the foremost seats, looking her usual self-possessed self, but she showed no consciousness of his regard. He saw, indifferently, a very tall, thin man, well though quietly dressed, who, having failed to obtain a seat, looked easily over the heads of others, as he stood in a gangway at the rear of the court.... He became aware that Mr. Dunkover had risen, and was addressing the magistrate.

"My instructions are," he was saying, "that certain additional information has come into possession of the police during the last few days which has an important bearing upon the prisoner's position, and, in the result, they do not propose to proceed further with the present charges. I ask therefore that the prisoner may be discharged."

Mr. Garrison considered this. "I think, Mr. Dunkover," he said, "I ought to know rather more than that."

Mr. Dunkover was still sparing of words. "I have advised," he said, "that it is a case, as it now stands, on which no jury would convict."

Mr. Jellipot rose with an unusual agility. "I must protest," he said. "I ask for my client's release not because the case against him would be hard to prove, but because he is an absolutely innocent man."

Mr. Dunkover, after a whispered consultation with his instructing solicitors and Inspector Combridge, rose to say: "My friend is entitled to say that; which the prosecution does not dispute."

Mr. Garrison rubbed his chin. He saw that there was more here than he was intended to know, which he did not like. He preferred to have reason for what he did. But after that moment's silence, he said no more than: "Very well. The prisoner is discharged."

It meant no freedom for Francis, who was hurried back to the cells. Before he was removed from the dock, he had observed that Inspector Combridge had already risen, and left the court by a side-door.

The movement had no significance for him, nor for a man who was more directly concerned. But, a moment later, the Inspector re-entered at the back of the court. He approached Mr. Entwistle from behind. That gentleman had made no motion to leave. His gaze passed over the court, now astir in the momentary interval before the next charge was called with the movements of those who had risen to leave, as though he were looking for someone who was not there.

It appeared that he had no intention of going himself, for he was about to occupy a vacated seat when Inspector Combridge touched him upon the arm.

"May I have a word with you?" he asked.

Mr. Entwistle looked surprised. He said shortly: "Yes. What is it?"

The Inspector answered quietly: "If you will come with me—we can't talk here."

Mr. Entwistle frowned. He looked displeased and hesitant. But he controlled himself to say nothing. He rose and went out with the Inspector, whose hand rested lightly upon his arm, in a way which he would not appear to observe, though he did not like it.

When they were in a small adjoining room, with two uniformed constables at the door, Inspector Combridge said: "Peter Entwistle, it is my duty to arrest you for the wilful murder of William Rabone; and I have to warn you that anything you say may be used against you in evidence."

The accused man maintained his calmness of voice and manner, though he could not control the blood that had left his face.

"I can only say," he replied, "that the charge is an absolute surprise to me. I know nothing about the murder beyond what I have read. Why, I never even—" He checked himself and added only: "I reply that I am not guilty. You should know well enough that—"

He checked himself in mid-sentence again. He had often imagined such a moment as this, though it had not been a charge of murder which he had then expected to hear. But he had not supposed that he would twice come near to saying such foolish things.

Later in the day, he was brought before the magistrate, and formally remanded for seven days, by which time it was understood that the police would be prepared to open their case.

CHAPTER TWENTY-TWO

Mr. Jellipot played a bold card. He briefed Rossiter to apply in Chambers for bail for Francis Hammerton (convicted in the name of Harold Vaughan) pending the hearing of his appeal.

Mr. Justice Fordyce heard the application with the patient immobility of expression due to an eminent counsel who was making the best of an impossible plea.

Even when he heard that Sir Reginald Crowe was prepared to provide bail to any amount which he might require, he did not allow any trace of the surprise he felt to appear.

He asked laconically: "*Any* amount, Mr. Rossiter?"

"Yes, my lord. Those are the instructions I have received. Sir Reginald will stand surety for any amount which you may require."

He conferred for a moment with Mr. Jellipot, and said again that there was no limit to the amount of bail which would be forthcoming.

For the first time a momentary doubt passed through the Judge's mind as to what his decision was going to be. He remembered that the bank inspector of whose murder the convict had been accused had been in the employment of the London & Northern Bank, of which Sir Reginald was chairman, and he saw that there might be more here than the surface showed. "You say, Mr. Rossiter," he asked, and his tone revealed the doubt that had come into his mind, "that your client's liberty is essential to the preparation of his appeal?"

"It is of the utmost importance."

Mr. Justice Fordyce was silent for one pregnant moment, during which even Mr. Jellipot's cautious temperament felt that the battle was won, but after that he shook his head slightly.

"I am sorry," he said, "but I see no sufficient reason for granting the application which has been so ably and eloquently made. You can renew it on Friday, if you think it worth while to do so. Yes, Friday. Eleven-thirty."

Mr. Rossiter and Mr. Jellipot withdrew without further words, and the legal gentlemen whose application was next on the list entered the room.

"You may congratulate your client," Mr. Rossiter said, "on the fact that he will be able to spend the week-end in his own home."

"You mean that he will grant bail on Friday?"

"You may expect that with some confidence."

As Mr. Rossiter foretold, so it proved to be.

On Friday morning the application was formally renewed, and Mr. Justice Fordyce asked no questions at all. He said, in his toneless manner: "Bail will be granted on Hammerton's own recognisances, and one surety for two thousand pounds, whose name must be approved by the court. Sir Reginald Crowe? Yes, certainly. You can have the order drawn up at once."

Mr. Rossiter, who had heard no more than he had had good reason to expect, he having busied himself during those two intervening days in ways which are not recognized by the law, but by which the cause of justice is often served, said: "Thank you, my lord"; and Mr. Jellipot had cause, for a second time, to feel that he had won success in the unfamiliar branch of litigation in which he moved. But he knew that the most difficult fence—the appeal itself—lay ahead.

Still, he had won a battle, if not a campaign, and it had been one which many more experienced criminal lawyers might have hesitated to try; and by so doing he had gained the ground for future strategic movements which it was essential to have.

Having won this success, he did not fail to take the full advantage which it allowed. He knew that time was the vital factor of the position, and he acted with such promptitude that, with Sir Reginald's equal diligence, it became possible, while the afternoon was still young, to open the prison doors, and Francis found himself leaning back in the comfort of Sir Reginald's private car, as it bore him smoothly, and at the best pace that the London traffic allowed, in the direction of Mr. Jellipot's office.

His sense of recovered freedom during this journey might have been more absolute had not Inspector Combridge been his sole companion. He was too ignorant of such procedures to do more than make a mistaken guess as to why the Inspector should be still at his side, or of what limited amount of freedom would now be his. At the best, he supposed that the Inspector was now beside him as one who would make formal delivery of his body at the lawyer's office. He wondered what would happen if he should ask the chauffeur to pull up, saying that he had decided to get out and go to his home by a different way.

Inspector Combridge, unaware of these thoughts, was making some honest efforts toward a friendly understanding. He commenced upon several indifferent topics of conversation, without gaining more than monosyllabic answers. The fact was that he still doubted the degree of that innocence about which Mr. Jellipot protested so strongly, and this uncertainty, of which Francis had an instinctive perception, was a bar to any real cordiality, even had he not embodied, to his companion's mind, the hated shadow of hostile law.

Yet it is bare justice to the Inspector to observe that he was not unwilling to be convinced, and he was as sincerely anxious to know the truth as he was genuinely endeavouring to establish friendly relations with his silent companion; for the point might be of vital importance to the soundness of the plan of campaign which was now to be discussed in Mr. Jellipot's office.

CHAPTER TWENTY-THREE

Francis found that the Inspector did not take his departure when he had (as he conceived the position) delivered his body to Mr. Jellipot.

Instead of that, he took a seat in the lawyer's office, without waiting for the formality of an invitation, while Mr. Jellipot, not appearing to observe this familiarity, was introducing Francis to another gentleman who had been seated on the farther side of his desk.

"This, Sir Reginald," he said, "is Francis Hammerton.... Mr. Hammerton, this is Sir Reginald Crowe, through whose kindness I have been able to procure your release."

Francis saw a man who looked young to be the chairman and actively controlling head of a great bank. His expression was of a dynamic energy, suggesting that his financial operations would be conducted with enterprise rather than caution as their dominant characteristic; as had, indeed, been the case since Lombard Street had been staidly stirred by the news that he had obtained control of a majority of London & Northern shares, and intended to use the voting power thus acquired to place himself in charge of the operations of the bank.

Sir Reginald looked at the young man who was thanking him rather shyly for the generosity which had procured his freedom. Accustomed to judge of the characters of those he met with a quick glance, which had rarely failed to guide him aright, he thought: "Jellipot right as usual. Jury must have been fools. Nothing strange in that." He said aloud: "You needn't thank me

too much. It's cost me nothing. I know you won't run away....
Besides, I'm wanting something from you; so the boot may soon
be on the other leg.... Tell him, Jellipot. You'll explain better
than I should."

He leaned back in the low leather chair he occupied, leaving
Mr. Jellipot to take the stage.

The lawyer began in his hesitant, precise manner, but with a
clarity of statement which made listening easy.

"We wish you to appreciate, Mr. Hammerton, the exact
position in which you stand, and the conditions on which your
permanent release, and the vindication of your reputation
depend.

"The Court of Appeal will have your case before them in a
fortnight's time from today. We have fourteen days. During that
time we must obtain further evidence, such as they will consent
to hear, or I am bound to advise you that the appeal will almost
certainly fail.

"The powers of the Court of Appeal, as it interprets them for
its own guidance, are extremely limited.

"It will not reverse a jury's decision on points of fact, unless
it should be of a most obvious perversity, even though it may
recognize that a different verdict would have been more consonant with its own conclusions. It will not consider evidence,
however relevant, which the defendant deliberately, negligently,
or perhaps by some miscalculating duplicity, withheld from the
lower court.

"It will interfere only on points of law, or on misdirections
of the Judge, or irregularities on the part of the prosecution, by
which a fair trial was denied to the accused.

"In such cases, it may even quash the conviction, in the interests of abstract justice, though it be an obvious consequence
that the guilty will go free.

"Finally, it may consent to hear evidence which has come
into possession of the defence since the date on which the trial
was held, and which reasonable diligence on their part could not
have obtained at that time.

"In this last is our best, and, in my judgement, our only hope.

"We cannot anticipate to succeed by submitting facts which you deliberately withheld, whatever motive you may have had; neither can we hope to argue convincingly that the jury, on the evidence which was before them, had no reasonable ground for the conclusion to which they came.

"What I feel that we require, and what I am therefore about to ask you to use your best efforts to obtain, is some fresh evidence—some new witness, if possible—whom you could not previously have called.

"It may not be easy—it may not be possible—but it is not a case of choosing between conflicting alternatives. It is the sole chance that your own indiscretion, if I may say so without offence, has left.

"To give you the greatest possible freedom of action, we have gone to some trouble to ensure that there will be no allusion in the daily press to the bail which has been granted to you. In looking up any of the acquaintances who were in any way responsible for your present position, or who would know you by your adopted name, you will be able to use the advantage of surprise; or you will be able to leave them in ignorance of your recovered liberty, if, in any case, you should desire to do so.

"There is a question which Inspector Combridge has raised, to which I am unable, from anything you have told me, to supply the answer, and concerning which even you yourself may have no certain opinion; but its importance is obvious.

"You were convicted as Tony Welch's associate. Tony Welch has, I understand, been known to the police for many years as a prominent member of an international gang of card-sharpers, confidence-tricksters, and negotiators of forged bonds, and other financial paper of illicit descriptions. You consorted with several members of this gang, whose true characters we are satisfied that you did not know.

"The question is, did they regard you as one of themselves, or as Tony Welch's dupe? If you go back to them, will they regard you as a fellow-criminal, endeavouring to avoid the punishment due to your guilt, or will they suppose that you were an innocent dupe, who will now have learnt, by a very bitter experience, to know them for what they are, and who is probably seeking both vindication for himself and their own exposure? I ask you to consider carefully before you reply, for you will see that the course of action which it may be prudent for you to take—even your personal safety—may depend upon the accuracy of your judgement upon this issue."

Mr. Jellipot paused upon this lengthy and lucid statement, the substance of which Sir Reginald or the Inspector might have put into a question of twenty words, and Francis, though it had allowed him ample time for consideration, was not ready in his reply. The question was not new to his mind. He had considered it in the ample leisure which is allowed to imprisoned men, but the answer was hard to find.

He said: "Augusta Garten knew. I think she tried to warn me once, but I wouldn't see. She couldn't have said much more than she did, without giving her own people away. But I thought she was trying to put me off for other reasons from going with her that night, and I took it all in the wrong way."

Inspector Combridge interposed sharply: "You could swear to that?"

"Yes.... I mean it's true, or I shouldn't have said it. Why do you ask that?"

"Because it confirms what we were nearly sure of before. We actually had a warrant made out at one time for that woman's arrest, and then decided that the evidence wasn't quite sufficient to get us home. We know how strong a case has to be against a girl with her looks. But if you could swear to that, it would show that she was aware what was on foot, and it might just be enough, with what we've got, to put her where she belongs."

Francis looked troubled. He said: "I shouldn't like to do that. It wouldn't be very decent, when she was trying to keep me clear of the mess."

Mr. Jellipot, observing a side-issue which might not be helpful, interposed before the Inspector was ready with his reply.

"Shall we keep to the present point? You think Augusta Garten understood your position, but, beyond that, you're not sure?"

"No. I should say some may have thought one thing, and some another. Those who were about with us most must have had some warning not to talk before me. At any rate, I never heard anything to lead me to think what they really were."

"That," Mr. Jellipot said, "seems to answer the question." He turned to the Inspector to ask: "How does it look to you?"

"If you ask me," Inspector Combridge replied, "I shouldn't say it goes far. The type of gangster with whom Hammerton got mixed up doesn't open his mouth to put his foot into it, even when he thinks he's among those of his own colour. I've been told by a man we had among them for over two years before they guessed what his business was, that even when they're planning a kill they won't say anything to each other that mightn't pass between respectable people, and they always talk as though the pretences they make to their victims are the solid truth they profess them to be to him. I suppose it makes the illusion easier to sustain, besides avoiding the risk of anything going into the wrong ears.

"Even if one of them had said something dangerous, and Mr. Hammerton had given him a blank stare in reply, he wouldn't have thought that he wasn't being understood. He would have thought that he was having a plain hint to keep his mouth shut by someone more discreet than himself."

"I think," Francis interposed, with more certainty than he had spoken before, "that some at least of them would take for granted that I was guilty, especially after the jury had come to the same conclusion. I don't think that even Moss & Middleton thought that I was really ignorant of what had been going on, though they defended me on those lines."

"It was a defence," Mr. Jellipot commented, with his mild-mannered acuteness, "which incidentally—and perhaps more than incidentally to their minds—assisted that of their principal client. In fact," he added, professional indignation raising his voice somewhat beyond its usual pitch, "you were very badly represented, or you would not be in your present predicament."

"I expect I was. They seemed shrewd enough, in their own way, and they always seemed confident they would get me off, but they weren't men it was easy to like. But I had no choice, really, especially as Tony was paying the bill.... I suppose you want me to look up his friends, and get someone to say that he knew Tony was making a fool of me. It doesn't sound very easy to do."

"I should put it," Mr. Jellipot replied, "rather more widely. You should be alert for anything which might have influenced the jury's decision had you been able to put it before them, without supposing in advance what it may be.

"I want you," Sir Reginald added, "to go farther than that. I want you to endeavour to find out anything which is being said in those circles about Rabone's murder, and most particularly anything which would connect Entwistle with it, or show that the two men had been associated, probably with others, in the criminal practices in which we suppose them to have been engaged. Or equally, of course, to learn anything that might tend to show that Rabone was killed because he was on the point of discovering a crime in which he was not involved himself."

Francis Hammerton considered these proposals with something less than enthusiasm, even though he reminded himself of the debt of gratitude he owed to those who had put them forward, and the position in which he stood.

"In fact," he said bluntly, "you want me to obtain their confidence by pretending that I was properly convicted, but have managed to wriggle out on bail, and then to betray it."

He had Augusta Garten in mind as he spoke, and his tone added to the effect of his words, to which his three auditors reacted in characteristic ways.

"You should not forget," Inspector Combridge said, with a feeling that his own profession was implicitly slurred, and yet conscious that, for the first time, he had really believed in

Hammerton's innocence as he spoke, "that you are dealing with murderers and professional thieves. If they make war on society, they can't expect it not to resist."

"My own hesitation," Sir Reginald said, "was on different grounds. Rabone's fate, if we are right as to what occurred, shows that we are dealing with men who will have little scruple in what they do, if their own safety should be at stake. It appeared to me that we were asking you to undertake an extremely dangerous, as well as difficult task.... But, of course, if you feel like that—"

Mr. Jellipot, who felt that Sir Reginald was concluding in the wrong way, mildly but firmly interrupted his valuable, but sometimes headstrong client: "May I say, Mr. Hammerton, that I think, with all respect, that your conclusions go somewhat beyond the logical implications of any proposals which either Sir Reginald or myself have offered for your consideration.

"I proposed that you should commence your enquiries with an absolutely open mind, and, beyond that, I suggested the possibility of your obtaining a witness in your support, who must, of course, come forward willingly, so that the question of your betraying anyone would not arise.... As to Sir Reginald's request, it is not suggested that your previous friends were concerned in William Rabone's murder, or even in the crimes of which it was a possible consequence, though we may have reason to think that they were sufficiently associated with those who were to know more about it than we have yet been able to learn."

"Well," Francis replied, overborne by his own thoughts, and the impact of these various arguments, "I don't want you to think me ungrateful for what you've done, nor insensible of the value of your advice. And as to anything being dangerous, if you ever get into such a position as mine, though I don't suggest that that's possible—well, you'll know that it isn't easy to care.... Yes, I understand, and you can rely on me to do what I can."

He rose as he spoke, as though to leave an interview which had reached its natural conclusion, and the movement roused Inspector Combridge to an equal activity.

He drew an oblong slip of paper from his pocket-book.

"Before you go," he said, "I must give you this. It's nothing to be afraid of, but you mustn't fail to be there."

Francis took it, and observed that it was a subpœna to attend as a witness, at ten A.M. on the following Monday, in the case of Rex v. Entwistle, at the Magistrates' Court.

CHAPTER TWENTY-FOUR

For a few hours, Francis found his mind distracted from the more difficult problems which must confront it, by the immediate necessity of obtaining shelter, and a larger portion of the elementary requirements of life than his pockets held.

The money which he had had at the time of his last arrest had been restored to him, together with a smaller sum, and other miscellaneous articles which he had had when first arrested at the Tipcat Club. He now provided himself with a suitcase of some solidity, and a sufficient quantity of linen and other articles to supply his needs for the fourteen days which seemed too likely to be the total measure of liberty that Mr. Jellipot's legal efforts would be able to gain.

Remembering the subpœna his pocket held, he observed that the privacy of his release, which Mr. Jellipot's caution had secured, was not likely to continue beyond the coming Monday. He supposed with some reason that it would be difficult for him to give evidence in such a case, and to leave the witness-box without his true name and present circumstances becoming almost universally known.

Well, he had two days. He could not call it more, for he had to be at the court at ten on Monday morning, waiting till he should be called to the witness-box. What could he do in so short a time? With no clear purpose in his mind, he decided to visit the Tipcat Club that night, where he had first met the acquaintances who had wrecked his life. He must be guided then by whom he would meet, and by the course of his conversation with them.

He might see Augusta Garten there, in whom was his best hope.

If she were not there, he decided that he would call upon her in the morning at the flat in Sheldon Gardens to which she had invited him (with others) more than once in the days when the seeking of her society was the first object that ruled his life. He would call at an hour when she might not be up, she being of those who sacrifice day for the darker hours; but it was unlikely, at such an hour, that they would be disturbed by such of her friends as he would not desire to meet. If he should see her at all, there would be time for conversation which would be unhurried, and might be unknown to any except themselves.

So he planned. But when he called on Inspector Combridge at the following noon, to fulfil a promise that he would report his address to him, he had a tale of double failure to tell.

As to the Tipcat Club, there had been a strange porter at the door, who regarded him with a suspicion which did not lessen when he gave a password several weeks out of date. Even when he abandoned the pretence of secrecy—he had commenced by giving his own name—and announced himself as Harold Vaughan, it was of no avail. The door was closed in his face, and there was no response when he continued for some minutes stubbornly pressing the bell.

He accepted this rebuff without much discouragement, as it was the second part of his programme in which he had better hope; but when he called at the Sheldon Gardens flat he found that Miss Garten's name had been removed from the signboard at the stair-foot. Miss Garten's flat was to let.

He sought the caretaker in the roof, and was informed that the lady had left a few days before. She had said that Scotland was her destination. Nothing more definite than that.

Had she left no address to which letters could be forwarded? No, she had not. But the woman, who was neither unfriendly to himself, nor disposed to regard him as one whom a young lady would go far to avoid, added that as Miss Garten had been receiving letters up to the morning when she somewhat abruptly left, and as there had been none arriving subsequently, she supposed that the post office had been instructed to re-address them. Probably, therefore, a letter would reach her.

Holding stubbornly to a poor hope, Francis waited at the foot of the stairs till the postman appeared. The man was civil, but not communicative. He admitted that he knew that Miss Garten had left. As to her letters being re-addressed, it was a matter between her and the post office, on which he was unable or unwilling to give a definite answer. If a letter were addressed to her, and were not returned, its delivery could be safely assumed.

Francis narrated to the Inspector the poor tale of his first day's experiences in the occupation which had been thrust upon him, supposing that he must incur the contempt which the expert may be expected to feel for the amateur's bungling efforts. But he was surprised to be met with sympathetic and encouraging words. The detective, who did not think it necessary to say that he was already familiar with most of the facts he heard, Francis having been unobtrusively watched from the moment when he had left Mr. Jellipot's office, approved the frankness of the account he received, and was aware that it is by a plodding persistence that the best results are obtained in the difficult profession to which he belonged. He recognized in Francis Hammerton a character of quiet obstinacy in which he had more confidence than he would have felt for more spectacular qualities.

More valuable than an abstract approval, he suggested a method by which Miss Garten's address might be obtained, even against her will.

"You can't hope to find her," he said, "on the information you've got. All you know is that she isn't in Scotland, to which we can add that she hasn't gone overseas, and the whole of England and Wales is a vague address with which to begin.

"If you send her a registered letter to Sheldon Gardens, the post office will re-address it, if they've got instructions to do so, but she isn't bound to reply, in which case you're no more forward by that. But if you pay an extra fee for the post office to give you proof of delivery, which they will do with a registered letter, providing it isn't refused by the addressee, the delivery slip will bear the actual address at which the letter is taken in.

"You'd better get a note off at once. If she answers, you might hear from her by Tuesday morning, and if she doesn't, you're quite likely to get an address by which you can follow her up.... But the fact is that the whole gang's rather scattered about. They all get flurried when we make a pounce, and go off different ways, so that it's as difficult as possible for us to keep track of them. It's like a cat getting a pigeon. The other birds fly off in a dozen directions, and most of them stay for a time on the roofs, though they've got to come down again, sooner or later, to where the corn's scattered about.

"Well, don't give up. You'll be surprised how far you get, if you go on one step at a time."

Francis thanked him, and went back to his room to write a note to Augusta Garten through which he hoped to have the uncertain pleasure of meeting a lady by whose attractions he had fallen into his present predicament.

CHAPTER TWENTY-FIVE

Mr. Dunkover appeared again for the Crown. Mr. Huddleston, K.C., assisted by Mr. Augustus Pippin, represented the accused.

Mr. Garrison, observing the eminent counsel who were to defend the accused, understood that it was not to be a case in which he would reserve any defence which he might be able to make until he should appear before the higher tribunal. The battle was to be joined at once, and seeing this, he made a quick mental revision of the time which he had calculated would be sufficient for dealing with it. Three days—possibly more. If both sides were prepared to go straight ahead, it meant a busy time for him during the coming week.

He glanced with professional interest at the second man whom the police had put into the dock to answer the present charge. No doubt the right one this time. Inspector Combridge didn't often make a mistake. The man didn't look like a murderer. But then, murderers seldom do.

He listened patiently to Mr. Dunkover's opening statement, and to the routine preliminary evidence. It was as necessary as it was boring. But he could trust his clerk to see that no essential was overlooked: that the depositions would be all that would be required by the higher court. He only became more than outwardly alert when Sir Lionel Tipshift entered the box to describe the injury which had been inflicted on the deceased, and to theorize on how it could have been caused, as the expert is allowed to do.

It appeared that the razor which had been found lying by the body, and which was, by an almost certain presumption, the weapon with which the crime had been committed, had been used twice, and with such savage strength that the neck of William Rabone, which had been short and thick, had been more than half cut through. One of the cervical vertebrae had been actually grazed by the blade, though it had not been severed. Death must have been almost instantaneous.

He described, with sufficient technical detail, the evidence by which he confidently deduced that the first wound, which had commenced on the front and left side of the neck, had been inflicted by someone standing behind, and probably slightly to the left of his victim. Its direction, in view of William Rabone's own height, indicated a rather tall man. If it were a woman, she must have been of unusual physique. The second wound had been inflicted, in his opinion, after the injured man had already fallen forward upon the floor.

"Would it have been possible," Mr. Dunkover asked, "for a man so wounded to have uttered a cry which would have penetrated to a lower floor of the house?"

"It would have been possible after the infliction of the first wound, but not the second. The wounded man appears to have staggered forward two or three paces toward the door, possibly with a blind instinct of escape, before he fell. After he had done so, his assailant must have bent over him and inflicted the second wound.

"Such a cry would have been uttered, if at all, during the moment before he fell."

"From the nature and direction of the wounds, can you say with certainty that they were not self-inflicted?"

"Yes. I have no doubt at all."

"Can you assist the court with any further deduction as to the assailant, or the course of the crime?"

"Only that there is a strong presumption that it was the work of a left-handed man."

"Thank you, Sir Lionel."

Mr. Dunkover sat down, and Mr. Huddleston rose to cross-examine the witness.

"You have expressed the opinion, Sir Lionel, that this is a case of murder, not suicide?"

"Yes. There can, in my opinion, be no reasonable doubt."

"Should you express that opinion with equal confidence, if it should appear that William Rabone may have had a very serious reason for self-destruction?"

"I should still hold that opinion."

"But you would not say—as I understand you do not say even now—that it is definitely impossible that the wounds may have been self-inflicted?"

"Not impossible, perhaps. I should call it a fantastic rather than an impossible theory."

"Do you base that opinion, partly at least, upon the extent of the wounds?"

Mr. Huddleston asked the question in a quiet and casual tone, knowing inwardly that it was the one hope that he had of shaking the effect of the witness's evidence, if he should oblige him with an affirmative answer. But Sir Lionel was too wary, and too sound in his surgical knowledge, to fall into the trap.

"On the nature," he answered, "not the extent."

There followed a long discussion between the learned counsel and the expert surgeon upon the nature, position, and extent of suicidal wounds, which need not be recorded in detail. Textbooks on forensic surgery were passed to the witness, and passages debated as bearing upon the evidence already given. But Sir Lionel's arguments remained unshaken.

Mr. Huddleston had not expected any other result. He knew that there was no reasonable doubt that it was a case of murder with which they dealt, though he had a very confident hope that he would be able to keep his client out of the legal net which was being spread for his destruction.

But he knew that, as he prolonged the discussion, and raised every side-issue the facts allowed, that there was a constant possibility that something of real or apparent inconsistency would be said, such as could be used at the subsequent trial to shake the jury's confidence in the witness, or otherwise confuse their minds.

Sir Lionel, who understood the game perfectly well, fenced adroitly enough to foil Mr. Huddleston's subtlest attempts, and, at the end of half an hour's exchanges, counsel had done no more than to elicit that a man who has an inclination to cut his throat usually begins with two or three tentative superficial wounds, and then, as his frenzy of resolution grows, may strike with such savage force as to sever his neck, even from one side to the other. Not only so, but he may repeat the blows, time after time, either through a mechanical determination previously formed, or in a desperate effort to hasten the oblivion that delays to come. Counsel and surgeon agreed upon the authenticity of a recorded case in which a man had hacked at his own neck until the transverse process of the fifth cervical vertebra had been completely severed.

Sir Lionel admitted readily that the extent of the wounds was not in itself an argument against suicide. He even conceded, as an abstract proposition, that it might be considered an argument on the other side. But he held impregnable ground when he dwelt on their direction, from front to back; on the fact that, unlike those that are self-inflicted, the ends of them were deep and sharp; and on other features concerning which it was minute and lucid, in which they—and the second one in particular—differed from anything which would have been the work of the dead man's hand.

When he was at last permitted to leave the box, there was probably no one in that crowded court who doubted that it was a savage murder which was in process of investigation.

Those who watched with sufficient closeness, may have observed that counsel had avoided cross-examination on the question of whether the murder had been the work of a left-handed man.

Mr. Huddleston sat down, looking content, but it was an expression without certain significance. It might mean no more than that he had had a fat fee to induce him to defend in a hope-less case, and that he was prolonging it in such ways as his brief required.

Peter Entwistle had also listened to the evidence with an easy interest, as though it were of no personal importance, but that also was without significance to those who were murderers who have gone to sleep in the dock.

CHAPTER TWENTY-SIX

"I call Francis Hammerton."

Francis, who had been waiting in the witnesses' room, entered the court and the witness-box at the same time, not knowing what might have occurred already.

He had not reflected that he might be called to answer to his own name, and when, in the next instant, he was asked his address, there was a second's pause before he replied, "44 Addleston Terrace, S.W. 6," giving that to which he had the best right, but from which he had so unavoidably absented himself during recent weeks.

His mind, as he spoke, went rapidly over the consequences which the publication of his own name and address would have. How quickly would it bring his own relatives, to whom his disappearance must have been a strange, if not alarming event, round the doors of the court? He was glad to think that the address of the room he had now taken need not be mentioned. He would still have a retreat from surrounding voices, whether of friend or foe, of which none but Mr. Jellipot and the police would be aware.

He was conscious in the same instant that Mr. Garrison, who had seen him in the dock a week before, on the charge now to be faced by another prisoner, but then with a different name, gave him a quick questioning glance, and that the eyes of Mr. Huddleston, whose position of defending counsel he did not yet know, rested upon him sharply for a moment, and fell again to his brief.

Mr. Huddleston's mind had, in fact, hesitated on the edge of suspicion, observing that second's pause; but he reflected that many shy and respectable witnesses dislike giving their addresses in public, in such a case as that on which they were now engaged. Besides, had there been any real importance attaching to this question, the witness would surely have been coached already by the solicitors for the police. The very fact that the reply paused seemed to Mr. Huddleston's mind conclusive that there was none. In fact, he defeated himself by his own subtlety, as those of acute mind are often likely to do.

But the truth was that the prosecution had not gone over this witness's evidence with him at all. Inspector Combridge had relied upon the accuracy of the statement which he had made when first questioned. A still-lingering doubt as to the extent of his past innocence or present veracity had resulted in a decision to leave him in the witness-box to his own defence, and he would have been more interested than pleased had he been able to read the instructions concerning himself which Mr. Dunkover's brief contained. But if he could keep up his own end, he would find that the prosecution had no disposition to queer the pitch.

"Occupation?"

"Commercial artist."

"Mr. Hammerton, on the fourth inst. I understand that you were lodging at seventeen Vincent Street, the address where Mr. Rabone also had his rooms, and where he met with his death?"

"Yes."

"He occupied a room on the attic floor, and you were sleeping in one on the floor below?"

"Yes."

"And you were roused by a cry in the night? Will you tell the court in your own words what occurred, as far as your knowledge goes?"

"I was roused by a cry—a loud, horrible cry—which seemed to come from the floor above. I felt certain that something terrible had happened. I got out of bed, and switched on the light.

"Then I half dressed, and went out on to the landing. There was no sound"—he hesitated for one observable second and went on, "after the cry, and so—"

Mr. Dunkover interrupted him, seeing that counsel for the defence had observed that second's hesitation, and thinking that the question which would almost certainly be asked would come best from himself.

"Let us be clear on that. After the terrible cry you have mentioned, you heard no sound whatever until you went out on to the landing?"

Faced with this direct question, Francis had the wisdom to answer frankly, "I meant nothing more of a frightening kind. I had thought that I heard steps overhead."

"In the room where the crime occurred?"

"No. I couldn't have heard them there. It was the other room that was over mine."

"Very well. You thought that you heard steps in the other room. You went out on to the landing. What did you do then?"

"I listened, but heard nothing. The whole house seemed to be in absolute silence. I switched on the landing light, and went up the attic stairs. I felt I couldn't go back to my own room without finding out what that cry had meant."

He paused a moment, and was aware that the court had become as silent as those midnight stairs. The simple brevity of his narrative had had an effect of realism, causing those who heard to share the feelings which were recalled to his own mind. At that moment, there may have been no one there, conscious of what had lain in the room above, who doubted the truth of the tale they heard.

"You went up the stairs, and then—" Mr. Dunkover led him smoothly forward.

"I looked first into the room on the left, because the door was open, and the light on. The room was empty. I noticed that the window was open, and there was a strong draught blowing through."

"I believe that that room was tenanted by a young lady whom

you knew as Miss Jones?"

"Yes."

"But you say that she was not there. Had the bed been occupied? Did you notice that?"

"Yes. I remember noticing that the clothes were half on the floor, as though they had been thrown hurriedly off."

Mr. Garrison interposed to ask: "You are calling Miss Jones, Mr. Dunkover?"

Mr. Dunkover said that he was.

"I only asked because I do not recall that you mentioned her in your opening statement."

"I mentioned her under the name of Weston, Jones being one that she had assumed under circumstances that she will explain."

"Very well. Pray proceed."

Mr. Dunkover returned his attention to the witness. "You noticed that the bed had been occupied, and appeared to have been hurriedly left. What did you do next?"

"I crossed the landing to Mr. Rabone's door. I knocked, but got no reply. After a few moments, when I found that I could not wake him, I tried the door, which was unlocked. I opened it, and went a step or two in."

"It was in darkness?"

"Yes. There was a little light from the open door on the other side of the landing, but I couldn't see anything distinctly till I found the switch, which I couldn't feel at first.

"I saw Mr. Rabone's body lying on the floor before that, but I didn't know what it was."

"And when you had switched on the light?"

"I saw him lying on the floor, with his throat cut. There was an open razor lying near. I thought at first that he had killed himself, and then I remembered the cry I had heard, and thought that he had been murdered.... I think I was rather frightened for a moment. I remember looking round to see if whoever had done it was still there.

"Then I thought that someone ought to be called. I went down to the basement, and knocked Mrs. Benson up."

"Mrs. Benson being your landlady?"

"Yes."

"Let us go back for a moment. Before you left Mr. Rabone's room, did you notice anything more than you have said? Did you notice, for instance, whether the window of his room were open or shut?"

"No. I can't say that I did. I think it must have been open, because I remember how the draught blew through when I opened the door, but I can't say that I saw."

"Had the bed been occupied?"

"I can't say that I saw. I don't remember anything clearly, except the way that Mr. Rabone lay on the floor."

"But you said that you looked round to see if anyone else were there?"

"Yes. I did that, but I've no clear recollection of what I saw, except that I felt sure that I was alone."

"Then you can't say whether the bed had been occupied. Was Mr. Rabone fully dressed?"

"Yes."

"Very well. We must accept that you observed nothing clearly except the dead man. Then you went down to rouse Mrs. Benson. And after that?"

"I went round to Sefton Street, to call Dr. Foster. That was what she asked me to do."

"And is that, from first to last, all you know of the matter?"

"Yes. I think I've told you everything that I know."

"With no reservation of any kind?"

"No. I really know nothing about it, except how I found Mr. Rabone."

"Very well. That is all."

Mr. Garrison looked at the defending counsel. "Any questions, Mr. Huddleston?"

Mr. Huddleston rose slowly. He had an impression that the witness had given a substantially true account of the finding of the body of the murdered man, though he had a feeling also, instinctive rather than logical, in his experienced mind, that there was something in reserve which it might, or might not, be advantageous to bring to light.

He had no suspicion of the truth. No suspicion that Francis was the Harold Vaughan who had been convicted of active participation in a despicable fraud a mere fortnight before, or that it was he who had stood, a week ago, in the place now occupied by his own client, and charged with the same crime. This was an ignorance which may be traced to the extensive business carried on by those enterprising criminal lawyers, Messrs. Moss & Middleton, from whom he had received his brief. They were now represented in court by Mr. Richard Middleton, Junior, and by a clerk, neither of whom had been concerned in Harold Vaughan's, earlier trial, and to whom his face was unknown.

Mr. Huddleston knew that it is a dangerous thing to attack an honest witness in ways which may alienate the sympathy of the court; and, beyond that, the line of defence on which he ultimately relied left this evidence so entirely aside that, from his point of view, Mr. Dunkover was merely beating the air. But there were a few questions which must be asked.

"Do I understand, Mr. Hammerton, that, on the night of the tragedy, so far as you are aware, you yourself, and the two women of whom we have heard, were the sole occupants of the house, in addition to the dead man?"

"Yes. So far as I know. I didn't see anyone else."

"And of these, Miss Jones had gone—how and when and where we shall doubtless hear from herself, and Mrs. Benson was asleep in the basement, so that you were the first to come into contact with the dead man, and to give the alarm?"

"Yes."

"Thank you. I think that will do."

He felt that his question had sufficiently indicated, without emphasizing, the fact that the witness's account was uncorroborated, and that there was nothing but his own word to show that he had not himself drawn the razor across the throat of the murdered man.

Francis stepped from the box, feeling that the ordeal had been less than he had expected to face, but as he did so Mr. Huddleston became conscious of the presence of a solicitor's clerk at his elbow, who was urgent to gain his ear.

Francis observed him also, and recognized the man who had been engaged in his defence at the earlier trial, and who, in fact, had entered the court a moment before with no other purpose than to give a message to Mr. Richard Middleton in connection with a different case. Francis saw that Mr. Huddleston's eyes were now directed sharply upon himself. He saw him rise hurriedly, and address the magistrate.

"I may very probably wish," he said, "to ask the witness one or two further questions. I will defer them, with your permission, if you will allow him to be recalled at a later stage. May I respectfully suggest that he be directed to remain in court in the meantime?"

"Certainly, Mr. Huddleston. All the witnesses will, of course, remain until they have my permission to leave."

Mr. Garrison, aware of a position which he did not fully understand, was careful to speak in a general manner, but a moment later he gave a quiet word aside to the usher, which instructed that functionary to ask Inspector Combridge to see that Mr.—Hammerton—should not leave without the permission of the court.

Meanwhile, Mrs. Benson had entered the box. Her flustered evidence threw no additional light on the tragedy which had brought her apartment-house into such unwelcome notoriety, and would be tedious to record. She would have entirely escaped Mr. Huddleston's attentions, had she not persisted in alluding to Francis as "Mr. Edwards," in spite of the careful contrary instructions which she had received before entering the witness-box.

"The late Mr. Rabone was a bank inspector?" he asked genially. "In fact, a man of the highest respectability?"

"Yes, sir," she answered, responding to his friendly tone. "No one could ever say as he wasn't that."

"Had you had the slightest doubt of his character or respectability, you would not have let him rooms in your house?"

"No, sir. I've always been careful who I takes."

"So I have no doubt that you have.... And this Mr. Hammerton—or Mr. Edwards, as you appear to be accustomed to call him—you had found him also to be a satisfactory lodger? Had he been with you long when this sad event occurred?"

"No, sir. He only came in the afternoon before."

"He came the afternoon before! And no doubt you had satisfactory references? No? No references! Thank you, Mrs. Benson. That is all."

Mr. Huddleston sat down well satisfied that he had sufficiently discredited the principal witness that the police had yet put into the box. It might have little direct bearing upon the case—whatever it might prove to be—which his client would have to meet, but it all tended to prepare the atmosphere he required for the moment to which he was already looking forward, when he would take the extreme course of asking the magistrate to refuse the committal of the accused.

CHAPTER TWENTY-SEVEN

Miss Weston entered the witness-box.

She took the oath, and gave her name and address, with a cool self-possession which suggested to Mr. Huddleston's experienced glance that she might be a formidable obstacle to his client's freedom, if she should have anything damning against him to which she would be prepared to swear.

But Mr. Peter Entwistle looked at her, and was undisturbed. He could not recall having seen her previously, and he decided that she was not one whom he would quickly forget. Anyway, he had a defence, when the time to show it should come, by which he hoped to bring a more worried look on to Inspector Combridge's face than it now bore—and even now he did not appear to be particularly well-content.

Meanwhile Miss Weston was saying that she was employed by the Texall Enquiry Agency. In the course of her duties with them, she had taken an attic-room at No. 17 Vincent Street, in the name of Mary Jones, about two months ago.

"With what instructions did you go there?"

"I was to make the acquaintance of Mr. Rabone, and to endeavour to discover whether he were in any way concerned in certain events which had occurred at the London & Northern Bank, of which he was an inspector."

Mr. Garrison interposed: "Am I to understand that your agency was acting on the instructions of the bank, or for private interests?"

"For the bank, of course."

Mr. Garrison's face cleared somewhat at this reply, but he asked again: "Then do I understand correctly that William Rabone was under the suspicion of his employers in connection with irregularities at the branches of the bank at which his inspections were made?" He turned his attention to Mr. Dunkover as he went on: "And, if so, is it a matter which should properly be brought out in connection with the present charge?"

Mr. Dunkover replied that the magistrate understood the position correctly. He was afraid that the issue of the probity of the dead man could not be entirely avoided. It might even become a question of the first importance. But it was only right for him to say at this stage that the instructions which Miss Weston received did not necessarily convey any imputation against him. Certain irregularities had occurred—it might not be necessary to be more specific—the source of which it had become imperative to trace, and under such circumstances it might become an unpleasant necessity to scrutinize the records, and to direct enquiries of other kinds upon a number of officials who would normally be above suspicion, and most of whom must be innocent and upright men.

Mr. Garrison said, very well. He was quite sure that counsel would avoid any imputation—especially against a man who could no longer defend his own integrity—which was not relevant to the present charge.

The examination proceeded.

"You did, in fact, Miss Weston, establish a considerable degree of intimacy—using the word, of course, in a quite innocent sense—with William Rabone?"

Miss Weston's reply paused.

"I don't think," she said, "that the word intimacy would be quite accurate, however you use it. He was never in any sense confidential with me. He professed friendship—or something more. You may say that."

"May we say that you appeared to have won his affections, but that you had not advanced to a point at which his confidence was equally given?"

"I should put it differently. I should say he acted toward me as, under such circumstances, it was normal for him to do."

Mr. Dunkover perceived clearly that, whatever William Rabone's feelings may have been, on her side, Miss Weston's affections had not been won. He was conscious of a slight irritation at the exactness of definition that the witness required, when he had been endeavouring to do no more than to lead her smoothly over the unavoidable preliminaries to the point where her evidence became important to the present case.

But he was pleased to observe, without appearing to do so, that Miss Weston's evidence had already caused an interchange of whispered words between Mr. Huddleston and his instructing solicitor, and that the latter gentleman was now occupied in a similar colloquy with Peter Entwistle over the rail of the dock.

Evidently the suggestion that William Rabone might be shown to have been involved in some conspiracy to defraud the bank, whether or not he may have been already known to be of that character by the defence, indicated a line of attack proposing an illicit connection between their client and the murdered man, or even a possible motive for the crime, which they saw that they must be wary to meet.

Mr. Dunkover went on: "Perhaps it may be sufficient to say that your relations as a fellow-lodger with William Rabone reached a superficial familiarity, of which he would have taken some further advantage had he been permitted to do so."

As Miss Weston received this amended definition in a silence which might be taken for assent, he continued quickly: "And during this time is it correct to say that you occupied one of the two attic rooms which constitute the top floor of Mrs. Benson's house, and that William Rabone had the other?"

"Yes."

"And did that contiguity enable you to observe any unusual or suspicious circumstance?"

"The second night after I took the room, I heard a noise that sounded like someone coming cautiously over the roof, and then entering through the window of Mr. Rabone's room. Then

I heard voices in his room—his own and one other's, if not more—which almost at once became very low. I supposed that he had given a warning that my room had become occupied.

"He or they who had come left after about half an hour, very quietly. It was a dark night, and without opening my window, which I hesitated to do, I could learn nothing more, except that whoever had come returned across the front of my window—that is that they went in the direction of Windsor Terrace."

"And were these visits repeated?"

"The same thing happened again about three weeks later, but on that occasion they were so quiet that I did not wake until I heard voices, very low, in Mr. Rabone's room. I had kept my own window closed and bolted since I had known that men were liable to be prowling about the roofs in the night, but when I heard the voices I got out and loosened it, so that it would open without noise—it was a dormer window, opening from side hinges—and when a man came out of Mr. Rabone's window, and went back the same way as before, I opened it, and followed him as closely as I safely could without being observed.

"The night was cloudy, but not very dark. I could not see the man with any distinctness—he went faster than I, and got farther away as he went on—but I counted the windows, and was sure that he went in at No. 13."

"Beyond these singular incidents, did you observe or hear anything of an unusual nature prior to the day preceding the death of William Rabone?"

"No. Nothing till the evening before."

"And then? Will you tell the court what occurred in your own way?"

"Mr. Rabone came in earlier than usual—about six o'clock. It had been understood that he would do so, and that he wanted to talk to me. He had made it plain that he didn't want Mr. Hammerton to be there, and he went upstairs when Mr. Rabone came in, so that we had a long time alone.

"The conversation didn't go at all as I had expected it would. He said almost at first that he had found out who I was, and that

I was spying on him. He made out that he had known all along, though I didn't think that was true. But he didn't seem to care, or to resent it at all. He treated it more as a joke.

"He said that I had been wasting my time, and that he had written to the general manager of the bank. He said he was going to make him an offer, and if it were taken in the right way, he could save the bank many thousands of pounds, besides more worry than it was good for bank directors to have; but, of course, he wasn't going to do it for nothing.

"He said, anyway, that he didn't care. It would be their funeral, not his. Even if they wouldn't come to terms, they couldn't do more than dismiss him, and he was thankful to say that he wasn't poor enough to mind that. Whatever else happened, he would resign. When he found that they were putting people to spy on him, it was time to bring things to an end, which he meant to do.

"Then he went on to say that I needn't worry about the office again, as he was going to give me a better life than that of a common spy. He would go abroad, and begin to spend money, instead of working all the time, as he had been doing till then, and I could share his life, as he seemed to feel sure that I should be willing to do.

"Even when I raised difficulties, he seemed to think that I only stood out because I wasn't sure that he would do all that he said.

"On my side, I wanted him to say more than he would—he was too cautious, from first to last, to let me learn anything definite—and so, altogether, we talked for a long time without getting much further forward."

Mr. Garrison intervened: "I must be clear upon this. Do I understand that Rabone admitted to you that he had been party to conspiracies for defrauding the bank by which he was employed, which he would be willing to betray if he were to receive a sufficient reward, but not otherwise?"

"No. It wouldn't be right to say that. He admitted nothing. But it was implicit in all he said."

"And he recognized at the same time that he was threatened

with exposure? Did he appear to be in a mood in which a man might destroy himself to escape the consequences of his wrong-doing?"

"No. Not in the least. He appeared confident in his own position, and contemptuous of anything they could do."

"And you feel sure that that attitude was genuine, and not merely assumed?"

"Yes. I don't think there could be any doubt about that."

"Very well. Pray go on, Mr. Dunkover."

"And how did this conversation end?"

"I allowed it to appear that I was overcome by his persuasions, and inclined to agree. It was after midnight then. I think I was willing to say almost anything which would have ended the conversation. I proposed to give him a final answer in the morning."

"Did he agree to that?"

"No. He became very difficult. I think he became more doubtful of what I meant than he had been while I was holding him off more indefinitely. He was very shrewd in his own way, but he had an idea that any girl could be bought, or that he would be attractive to her, or perhaps both. He said he must have an answer then, and he made it very clear what he meant it to be.

"I said I was too tired to say more that night, and was going to bed. He didn't object to that, but he followed me up, and tried to come into my room before I could lock the door.... He'd tried to do that more than once before, but I'd had less difficulty in putting him off.

"Now he said that I'd got to learn that one room was enough for both, and I might begin then just as well as later. I threatened to call Mrs. Benson or Mr. Hammerton, if he wouldn't leave me alone for that night, but he said he didn't care about them. He knew how to manage them, and a few more if it came to that.... And then I happened to say, did he know how late it was?—that it was half-past one then, and when I mentioned the time he suddenly altered, and said he hadn't known that I was as tired as I said, and of course he'd wait till the next night.

"I felt sure it was reminding him of the time which had made such a sudden change, and it made me guess that he was expecting a visitor to his room of whom he didn't wish me to know, so I went into my own room, and locked the door, and loosened the window, and after a few minutes I put out the light, as though I had gone to bed. But I didn't really undress. I just lay down on the bed."

The magistrate interrupted again: "You say you lay down on the bed. You didn't open it?"

She thought a moment, before she replied. "Yes, I did open it. But I mean I didn't undress. I lay down in my clothes. But it was a cold night, and I drew the bedclothes over me. I think I had got chilly staying so long downstairs."

"You will see," Mr. Dunkover said, "that that supports the evidence we have heard already."

Mr. Garrison agreed. "Yes. It was a small point, but I wished it clear."

Miss Weston went on: "I think I dozed, though I hadn't meant to, for the next thing of which I was conscious was a murmur of voices in Mr. Rabone's room. It was low at first, but after that it became louder, and then low again, rather as though there had been a quarrel which had been made up, and then I heard Mr. Rabone give a terrible cry.

"I jumped up when I heard that, and ran to his room. As I crossed the landing, I remember seeing a line of light under his door, and hearing something that sounded like a struggle within the room. But as I was opening the door someone pressed against it from the inside, and then the light was switched off.

"After that, the door opened easily. I couldn't see anything inside, but I thought I heard something move on the floor, and a man's steps crossed the room to the window. I remember thinking that, though I could see nothing, I must be conspicuous to anyone in the room while I stood in the doorway, so I stepped in, and somewhat sideways while I felt for the switch. I couldn't find it for a moment. It isn't just where you'd expect it to be. And when I did get a light I saw a man's legs disappearing through the open window.

"The next moment, I saw Mr. Rabone on the floor. He was still moving, but you could see at a glance that he was beyond help. His head was—well, you could see.

"I switched off the light again. I don't quite know why. It may have been to conceal myself from the man who had just gone through the window, or it may have been to shut out the sight of Mr. Rabone on the floor. I just did it, without stopping to think.

"I slipped back to my own room, and opened the window. The man was evidently getting away as quickly as he could, and making more noise than I had heard the time before. I followed, but could not get near enough to see what he was like. In fact, he got farther away.

"But I saw him go in at the same window—No. 13—as before, and a minute after I crept quietly up to it, and looked in.

"It didn't open into a room, but an unlighted landing, with some stairs going down at the farther end. There was no light on the landing, but a little light came from the stairs. It shone up from the floor below. I looked in for a minute, and it was all quiet, so I tried the window. It didn't seem to have any fastening except a loose-fitting latch, and I had it open in a moment, without making any noise, and got down on to the landing.

"I thought that if I could get down to the front door and found it barred, it would almost certainly mean that the man was remaining within the house, and probably someone who lived there, but if the door were open it would mean that he had escaped into the street.

"I went down as quietly as I could, though it seemed that every stair creaked, but I heard no other sound, and I couldn't see any lights under the doors. The house might have been empty for anything I could tell. And when I got down to the street door, it was shut, but not bolted. It closed with a Yale lock, and when I pulled this back it opened at once.

"I looked out into the street, but there was no one there, and I stood for some moments undecided what I should do. I didn't feel inclined to go back into the house, nor to go to number seventeen, and have to knock Mrs. Benson up, and see Mr. Rabone again with her.

"I felt that it wasn't really my matter how he had got killed, and anyway I'd done all that I could, and the best thing I could do was to go back to my own home, and report to the office in the morning."

"You appear to have acted, up to that point," Mr. Garrison said, "with a good deal of courage, and some discretion, but you should have known that it was your duty to have informed the police at once. In such a position your first duty is to the state."

Miss Weston was conscious that her feeling had been at the time that her first duty was to her employers, and the doctrine stated with such assurance by Mr. Garrison is probably one to which the majority of women only conform when it coincides with more intimate codes. But if her mind did not accept this precept, she had sufficient sense not to question it. She said: "I've seen since that I didn't act very wisely; but I suppose I'd had about as much as I could stand for the time," and the magistrate accepted the explanation without further comment.

Mr. Dunkover said: "It appears that Miss Weston reported her experiences to her employers, who communicated with the London & Northern Bank immediately, and Miss Weston's statement was at once put at the disposal of the police."

Mr. Garrison made no reply. He had glanced at the clock which was on the opposite wall of the court, and observed that it was ten minutes to two. It was a tribute to the dramatic quality of Miss Weston's narrative that he had not previously observed that it was past his usual time for lunch. He said: "I think this will be a convenient time to adjourn. Till two-thirty prompt."

CHAPTER TWENTY-EIGHT

When the court reassembled, Mr. Dunkover announced at once that he did not propose to ask Miss Weston any further questions, and in the absence of Mr. Huddleston, who had not returned to the court, Mr. Augustus Pippin rose to cross-examine the witness.

Mr. Pippin was not an advocate of aggressive manner. He would seldom attempt to browbeat or bully when exerting his forensic skill to expose the mendacities in which those of the other side are supposed to revel.

He had a friendly ingratiating style of address, such as would have been called fatherly in an older man. He would discuss a witness's evidence with him in an intimate, confidential manner, as though uniting with him to bring into clearer light the facts distorted by the blundering questions of the previous advocate.

He was entitled, by the etiquette of the occasion, to undertake the questioning of at least one of the less-important witnesses, but it was a compliment to his reputation that Mr. Huddleston entrusted him with Miss Weston's cross-examination. He had actually hesitated between doing this and surrendering Francis Hammerton to his junior's seductive ministrations. But he was undecided as to the expediency of recalling Francis to the box, and he may have thought that Mr. Pippin's methods would be particularly well adapted to procure Miss Weston's undoing, if there should have been more or less than truth's simplicity in her fluent narrative of a night's adventures.

"Miss Weston," Mr. Pippin began, with a friendly glance,

approaching admiration, at a young lady on whom it was easy to smile, "I think you told us that you were in Mrs. Benson's house about two months?"

"Yes. It was about nine weeks."

"And you have explained very clearly the degree of intimacy (if you will permit the word) which had developed between yourself and Mr. Rabone during that time, before which he was, as I understand—in fact, he must have been—an absolute stranger to you?"

"Yes. So far as I know I had never seen him before."

"That was obvious, because, had you been previously acquainted, you would not have entered the house under an assumed name. You did so, as you have told the court, under that of Mary Jones. Would you please explain why?"

"I think I chose it because it was an easy one to remember."

"Yes. I suppose it is. But why change it at all?"

"I believe it is quite usual to do so when engaged in such enquiries."

"Possibly so. It is a matter on which I am not well informed. But what I am anxious to know is why it should have been done on this occasion."

"It may have obvious advantages."

"Yes. But it must have disadvantages also, which are at least equally obvious. You might be met by someone to whom you were known, who would use your true name in a disconcerting way. Or you might use or sign it yourself by inadvertence, so that the imposture would be disclosed. May I take it that it has been your habit to use an assumed name when engaged in such investigations?"

"It was the first time that I had had occasion to do so."

"You mean that it is the first time that you have been engaged in work of this kind?"

"Yes."

"How long have you been in the employment of the Texall Enquiry Agency?"

"About three months."

"And previously?"

"I had no previous employment."

"You are, perhaps, a young lady of private means?"

"I have a small income."

"And yet you engaged in this somewhat unusual and even, to some ways of thinking, repellent occupation. Do you mind saying why?"

"Well, it was something to do."

As Mr. Pippin asked these questions, his expression had been friendly, his tone casual. He had not appeared to notice that there had been increasing hesitation, if not actual evasion, in the brief replies he received, but it was clear to all who watched and listened that Miss Weston was replying with reluctance, and with a growing impatience hardly controlled.

Her last answer found Mr. Pippin in pleasant agreement.

"Yes," he said. "So it was. But it is not always easy, even for young ladies of, if I may say so, exceptional abilities and attractions, to get such positions without previous experience. How did you first get in touch with the Texall Agency?"

"I was introduced by Sir Reginald Crowe—by the London & Northern Bank."

Mr. Pippin paused for a moment, in an atmosphere which had become tensely silent with the instinctive realization that they were on the edge of one of those dramatic episodes in which a witness, giving evidence which may have been equally unexpected both to prosecution and defence, will sometimes confuse the issue for both alike, or destroy the very foundations on which they have united to build. His examination to this point had illustrated the soundness of Inspector Combridge's maxim that if you are content to go on a step at a time you may be surprised by the distance which you progress. He had commenced with a convenient opening from which he had intended to pass rapidly to a further and more promising line of attack, but he had perceived at once, with the sense, half instinct, half reason, of the practised advocate, that there was something held in the reserve of the witness's mind which it might be profitable to probe.

Now his tone became slightly expostulatory, as though in good-humoured protest at the defects of a woman's logic: "You were introduced by the London & Northern Bank! Shall we say that you were introduced for the explicit purpose of making William Rabone's acquaintance? And do you still say that you had no special reason to change your name?"

In a long moment of silence, and with visible effort, Miss Weston controlled herself to reply: "Whatever reason I may have had, it has not the remotest connection with the murder concerning which I am giving evidence, and I would prefer not to reply."

"I am sorry, Miss Weston, but I must still ask you to do so."

"I think it should be sufficient when I say that it has nothing to do with the present case."

"It is a matter on which you may not be the best judge."

Mr. Garrison interposed. "The questions appear to be quite simple, Miss Weston, and I must instruct you that it is your duty to answer them. It is very difficult to see why you should object to do so. I will repeat them for you. Did you enter the employment of the Texall Enquiry Agency with the direct purpose of being appointed to watch William Rabone? And why did you think it necessary for this purpose to change your name?"

It might be noticed by those who watched closely that Miss Weston's hands, which had been pressed tightly upon the rail of the witness-box, relaxed their tension, and her voice lost its previous tone of restraint, as she replied.

"Very well. If you insist, I must tell you. I did it I because I knew that Mr. Rabone was responsible for my father's death."

Mr. Pippin contrived to look several things at the same time. He was surprised, shocked, sympathetic, anxious for more. Inwardly, he was in excellent spirits, finding that he was reaping a fruitful crop from what he had expected to be lean if not barren ground. He began: "Perhaps, Miss Weston, you would—" But Mr. Garrison interrupted him.

"I will deal with this, if you please. Miss Weston, I am sure you realize the gravity of the allegation you have just made. Will you tell me what ground you have for charging William Rabone with responsibility for your father's death?"

"My father was chief accountant at the head office of the London & Northern Bank. He shot himself two years ago, after he had been transferred to a less responsible position."

"And how does that support the imputation against the man with whose murder—if such it were—we are now dealing?"

"The bank was the victim of certain forgeries of a very cunning kind, which required an inside knowledge such as my father had. He said that there was only one other man except himself who could have given the information by which those frauds were successfully carried out. That was Mr. Rabone. My father said to me, time after time, that he was sure Rabone was guilty, but that he had no proof, and that was not a thing which he could say, when there was equal suspicion against himself.

"He was never the same man after that incident, though he received a letter from the directors assuring him of their continued confidence. His health broke down, and that was, as I have since been assured, the only reason that he was transferred to a position of less responsibility. But he took it the wrong way, and he committed suicide two days later."

Mr. Garrison considered this explanation. He addressed Mr. Pippin: "You will see that Miss Weston felt that if it could be shown that Rabone was an unfaithful servant to the bank, it would clear any shadow of suspicion from her father's name. It is a matter which may or may not be relevant to the present case. At present, it seems to me to be somewhat remote. Perhaps that will be all, Mr. Pippin?"

It was a plain hint that, in the magistrate's opinion, the cross-examination should not be continued; but Mr. Pippin had been consulting hurriedly with Mr. Huddleston (who had re-entered the court a few minutes earlier), and he now rose to say that there were a few further questions which he felt it necessary to ask. "I have," he said, "my client's interests to consider."

"That," Mr. Garrison agreed, "is the paramount consideration. Go on, Mr. Pippin."

Mr. Pippin turned to the witness: "You have told the court, Miss Weston, that you accounted William Rabone responsible for your father's death, and having that conviction in your mind—whether it were well-founded or not—you were willing to be the instrument of his ruin?"

"I wanted to get the truth."

"Yes.... Whatever it might be?"

She considered this with a slight frown. "Yes. But I knew what it would be. You see, I had known my father."

"Anyway, you would have won William Rabone's confidence, if you had been able to do so, and betrayed it to his employers, if it would have resulted in his conviction for defrauding the bank?"

"Oh, yes," she answered. "He would have betrayed them first, would he not? That was what I intended to do." Her lips set firmly as she added, in a low voice, as though to herself, and yet so that it could be plainly heard through the silent court: "I would have done more than that."

Mr. Garrison looked up from his notes to regard the witness in a keenly questioning way. Mr. Pippin allowed a slight expression of surprise to pass over a face by which his thoughts were not often shown. Mr. Richard Middleton Junior murmured, "Perhaps you did," loudly enough to be heard by most of those on the legal benches, and by Mr. Garrison, who gave the solicitor a glance of silent but sharp rebuke.

Mr. Pippin asked: "And will you please tell the court exactly what you would have been willing to do?"

"I mean that he couldn't have got more than he deserved, or than I should have been glad to have been him have."

"Even to his death?"

She did not appear to observe the possible implication of her replies. She said: "I'm not sorry he's dead, if you mean that."

"Would it be correct to say that what you saw of him during the last few weeks did not lessen the hatred which you had felt when he was no more than the name of a man you had never met?"

"I think it made it worse. I hated him for what he had done, and I disliked him additionally for what I found him to be. I think that was how most people would feel."

"Perhaps they would.... And having these feelings, you would not be stirred to any animosity toward anyone who might kill him, nor desire to bring such a one under the penalty of the law?"

Miss Weston paused on this question. She glanced at the man in the dock, as the one to whom allusion was presumably made. Peter Entwistle did not look particularly repulsive to her. "No," she said. "Not the least. I think it's a better world now he's dead."

"Yet, having these feelings, you showed, on your own account, considerable courage, and ran into more possible danger than most young women would care to face, with no other object than to trace the murderer of the man whose death you regard as giving so little cause for regret. Can you explain that?"

"I didn't think of it in that way. I just wanted to get at the truth, as I had been doing all along." She added: "But if I had thought of it like that, I expect I should have done much the same. I should have thought they all belonged to the same gang, though they might have quarrelled among themselves."

Mr. Pippin was not sure that he liked this reply, and had sufficient discretion to see that if he continued further he might fare worse. He decided to switch off as rapidly as possible to another line of attack. He asked: "You are quite sure that you have told the court the full truth, neither more nor less, as to why you left your room immediately following William Rabone's death?"

"Yes. I am quite sure about that."

"And the man you followed—if there were actually such a man—you did not see, and could not identify?"

"No. I shouldn't recognize him at all."

"Very well. We must leave it there.... Now on another matter. You have told us how Rabone forced his attentions on you at a late hour of the night—actually at 1:30 A.M.—and how frightened you very naturally were, especially so, if I understand rightly what had occurred, because, up to a certain point, you had given him encouragement, or, at least, some reason to expect complaisance from you.

"At that time we may suppose that Mrs. Benson was fast asleep in the basement, three or four stories below. When you were on the top landing, or even when you were on the one outside Mr. Hammerton's door, she may have been out of hearing, but Mr. Hammerton certainly was not.

"If I understood you correctly, you threatened to call him to your assistance, but Rabone was, to use your own word, contemptuous of any interference from him, and you do not appear to have been surprised at this attitude.

"May I conclude that Mr. Hammerton, or Edwards as I believe that he was known to Rabone and yourself—or was it possibly Vaughan?—was previously acquainted with William Rabone, and presumably under his influence?"

"No, I think that is wrong. I believe they had only met on the previous day. I have really no doubt about it."

Mr. Garrison turned over his notes. "I think," he said, "we already have Mr. Hammerton's evidence to that effect."

Mr. Pippin said: "Yes. That is so," in a tone that I implied that the word of Mr. Hammerton, Edwards, or Vaughan, was of negligible value on any subject whatever. But Mr. Garrison was of a scrupulous impartiality. He was dubious about Mr. Hammerton in more ways than one, but the oath of any man is not to be lightly set aside, if there be no contrary evidence to weigh it down. He said: "Well, go on, Mr. Pippin."

"Then, if we are to accept the supposition that they were no more than acquaintances of a few hours, will you repeat Mr. Rabone's contemptuous words, as exactly as you can recall them?"

Miss Weston had a moment of silence, as though she searched a deficient memory for words which she could not recall with the certainty that the occasion required. In fact, she remembered them without difficulty, but she had some reluctance to quote them. They must be offensive to publish, and might be harmful, to one toward whom she felt as a friend. But she reflected that, from one angle or other, the facts would certainly be revealed concerning all who had been on the scene of William Rabone's death, and that a frank answer might ultimately be best, in more ways than one. She answered: "What he said was, as nearly as I can recollect, 'You'll get no help from that jailbird. Do you think he's going to call in the police?'"

"And you understood that singular allusion to Mr. Hammerton's past or present position?"

"Yes. I knew what he meant."

"Although, like Mr. Rabone, you had only made his acquaintance a few hours previously?"

"Yes. Mr. Hammerton had told me what had happened."

"You knew, in fact, that he was an escaped convict?"

"I knew he had escaped from prison."

"And you had no thought of informing the police?"

"No. I should have thought it would have been a very mean thing to do."

"Don't you recognize that it is the duty of every citizen to assist the officers of the law?"

"I thought Mr. Hammerton was an innocent and most unfortunate man."

Mr. Garrison allowed himself to smile slightly at this example of feminine logic, which Miss Weston evidently considered to be a sufficient reply. He said: "Don't you think we are going rather far afield, Mr. Pippin? I am not sure that I should not have warned the witness that she is not bound to answer your latest questions."

Mr. Pippin said he would leave it there, but before he could resume his examination Mr. Jellipot was on his feet.

"As representing Mr. Hammerton—" he began

"I am not sure," Mr. Garrison interrupted, "that I can hear you in that capacity."

"I think," Mr. Jellipot persisted, with a gentle firmness, "after what has been said already, that a few words of explanation may assist the court."

Mr. Garrison looked dubious. But he was himself considerably puzzled; particularly in respect of the fact that Francis Hammerton, an escaped convict of recent notoriety, and who had stood in the dock on a charge of murder a week ago, did not appear to be in the present custody of the police. He said doubtfully: "Well, a few words, Mr. Jellipot, if you assure me that it will assist the court."

Mr. Jellipot had the good sense to take the permission literally, and showed that he could be brief and pointed when the occasion required.

"I only wished," he said, "to make Mr. Hammerton's present position clear. It is true that he was recently convicted of a criminal offence, and that he escaped from the custody of the police. He has now appealed against that conviction, and has been granted bail until the appeal can be heard."

Mr. Garrison considered this, and felt more surprise than he permitted himself to show. He said only: "That is quite clear. I am obliged to you, Mr. Jellipot, for your assistance.... Pray continue, Mr. Pippin."

Mr. Pippin resumed: "You have said, Miss Weston, that William Rabone was a man you hated, as being, in your belief, ultimately responsible for your father's death. You were on the track of his supposed criminality, with the object of revenging yourself upon him. Up to the last day—almost up to the moment when you went upstairs together, as you have told the court, to the attic rooms where he was to meet a violent death in the next hour—you appear to have had a hope that you would be the instrument by which he would be brought to justice for the crimes which, rightly or wrongly, you believed him to have committed. But that evening that hope—that expectation— must have finally left your mind. You heard him express confidence that he could make terms with the bank which would be profitable to himself, or, at the worst, that they would be able to do no more than dismiss him, which he had no occasion to fear. Did you not realize, at that moment, that, unless you should take it into your own hands, and that instantly, your hope and opportunity of revenge might be gone for ever?"

Mr. Pippin's manner had altered as this last question was asked. His tone had become solemn, and tense with the accusation that it conveyed. Yet Mr. Garrison, listening carefully, recognized that it was put in a form to which no exception could be taken.

Miss Weston considered it for a moment, as though not instantly grasping whatever meaning it had. Then she gave Mr. Pippin a straight glance, as she said without apparent resentment: "What you want me to say is that I killed him myself, which is untrue."

"I want you to answer the question, which I will repeat if necessary."

"There is no need to do that. The answer is that I didn't think about it in that way at all."

"Very well. That is your answer. You didn't think about it in that way at all!"

Mr. Pippin sat down, and Mr. Garrison looked at Mr. Dunkover to ask: "Do you wish to re-examine the witness?"

Mr. Dunkover shook his head, and Mr. Garrison said: "Then we will adjourn at this point." He continued to address Mr. Dunkover when he asked: "I wonder how far you can help me as to how much further time this case is likely to need."

Mr. Dunkover said that he had one more witness to call. He did not anticipate that he would be long in the box. So far as he was concerned, the case might be over by noon tomorrow.

Mr. Huddleston rose at once. "When the prosecution have completed their case, unless they have some very different evidence from any which we have yet heard, I shall ask you to discharge Mr. Entwistle forthwith. Should you decide against me at that stage, I shall put my client into the box, and shall have at least three other witnesses to call. I anticipate being able to satisfy you of Mr. Entwistle's absolute innocence."

Mr. Garrison's face was expressionless as he replied: "Thank you, Mr. Huddleston. That was all that I wished to know."

CHAPTER TWENTY-NINE

Inspector Combridge left the court with a cheerful expression, not wishing his opponents to know how worried he really felt. He had seen that if he should get a committal, he would have much to do to complete his case to a point at which a jury's conviction would become tolerably certain, but that was a difficulty which he was used to meet, and to overcome.

But if Mr. Garrison should refuse to commit the accused man, it would be a rebuff to the police for which he would have the major responsibility. And he could not conceal from himself that it was becoming more than a possibility. It was not only that one of the two witnesses to the event which he had produced had been disclosed as a convict now actually under the sentence of the law, and the other as a woman who had been bitterly seeking revenge on the murdered man. More or less, he had been prepared for that, though he had not anticipated that Miss Weston's cross-examination would have developed quite as it had done. But he had discussed these difficulties with Mr. Dunkover, and they had agreed in considering them to be surmountable obstacles.

That which disturbed him most was the offensive confidence with which the eminent counsel secured by Peter Entwistle's ill-acquired money were conducting the defence: the talk of witnesses whose identity he could not guess, but who were to be brought forward to his confusion.

He saw that the defence must have some weapon in their armoury of the nature of which he was unaware, and that was worse than to be confronted by a difficulty, however great, which he could measure and understand.

He met Mr. Dunkover leaving the court, and saw a man as professionally unruffled, and inwardly almost as perturbed as himself. Mr. Dunkover also looked defeat in the face, and recognized that it would be attributed in legal circles to the abilities of the opposing counsel. Everyone knew (it would be said) that Dunkover was no match for Huddleston—and with Pippin against him also!

But if he feared the result, he was no less resolute to put up the best fight he could, and he pointed out what he thought to be a gleam of light on an otherwise darkened sky.

"You'll find," he said, "that Garrison won't be disposed to discharge the prisoner before he's gone into the box, and when we have him there, you never know what we may get him to say. If we'd been in this position before the date when accused men were allowed to give evidence on their own behalf, I should have said it looked a good deal worse than it does now.... Of course, Garrison knows that you wouldn't have put the man in the dock unless you'd been pretty sure that he'd fill the bill, and he'll give you every chance that he fairly can."

"Yes," the Inspector agreed, "I should say we can depend on him for that, but I wish I knew a bit more as to what their witnesses are going to say. You don't think there's any real doubt that we've got the right man this time?"

"I don't think the murder was done by either Hammerton or the young lady, if you mean that. I think they're both telling a straight tale, and, if so, the more they're attacked, the better we shall come off in the end, especially when we've got a jury to deal with.... But the trouble is that their evidence doesn't go quite as far as it should, and Bigland's hardly makes it up to a full weight.... But as to whether you've got the right man, I should say you've made a good guess, and if he didn't do it himself, he probably knows who did.... Well, it's no use worrying. I've been on a worse road before now, and got home in the end."

Inspector Combridge must take what comfort he could,

which was not much, from that guarded reply. If he had got the wrong man for the second time, he was likely to live in the records of Scotland Yard in a way which he had not anticipated, and certainly did not desire. He looked round for Francis Hammerton, to whom he had wished to speak, having a vague hope that, in his search for those who could support the plea of his own innocence, he might hear something of that in which he was less directly concerned, but Francis had already gone.

He had slipped away the moment that Mr. Garrison left the bench, fleeing to his unknown room from a publicity the extent and consequences of which he feared, but was unable to judge.

Had he stayed, he would have been able to tell nothing to the Inspector's comfort or his own advantage, for the weekend had been spent in abortive search for more than one of his old acquaintances who had left the city. He had gained no more than an increasing realization that the ways of the amateur detective are not easy to tread, and had resigned himself to the conclusion that he must succeed in getting in touch with Augusta Garten, or return to the prison walls from which he was so shortly and precariously set free. And even if he should see her again, who could guess what she would be likely to do or say?

If he had any comfort of mind for this night, it was in recalling the voice of a girl who had said, with a confidence very pleasant to hear: "I thought Mr. Hammerton was an innocent and most unfortunate man." But, unfortunately for him, Miss Weston was not one of the Judges of the Appeal Court.

He spent the evening in watching for a postman who did not come, having a faint hope that Miss Garten might answer by that time, and he left his room an hour before that at which breakfast could be obtained in the morning, seeking for a letter on the hall-table, and was only aware how faint his expectation had really been when he saw an envelope of the familiar mauve, addressed in Augusta's bold but insubordinate hand—for Miss Garten's handwriting had the curious quality that while it had its own regularity, it would decline to conform to the size of the paper on which she wrote.

He took the letter back to his own room before opening it, which cost him a needless climb up three flights of stairs, to be descended again in haste, for what he read was this:

DEAR HAROLD,

Why such a filthy trick? If I had not known your writing, I should have refused it, of course.

Not that there is any reason, but no one likes to be caught in a mug's trap.

Call up Ellerton 6603 within a quarter of an hour of when you get this, and we'll have a few words.

A. G.

He had discretion enough to avoid the telephone in the hall, and went out to seek a street instrument, which he found in three minutes of brisk walking. He rang up the number mentioned, and heard Augusta Garten's voice answering.

"You needn't tell me who you are," she said quickly. "I know that well enough. You know the restaurant in the side-street off Piccadilly, where we met once or twice before? There's no need to mention it, if you do.

"If you go there about seven tonight, and straight upstairs, and come in at the second door on the right, you may find me there, or you mayn't. It depends.

"But look here, Harold, you mustn't mention to anyone that you've rung me up, or that I'm going to see you again. I don't mean who you think. I mean anyone. Just what I say. Promise? Very well. It'll be your loss if you do.

"That's enough now. You're certain you know the place? I've no time to chat."

He had no time to thank her before she had rung off, leaving him to puzzle out what these instructions might mean.

Her letter, though it had no address at its head, certainly implied that she was not in hiding, and had nothing to fear from the police, to whom she had also alluded plainly enough when she had said, "I don't mean who you think." And to give a telephone number is to give a means by which you may be as quickly and certainly traced as by the fullest postal address.

She had told him to ring her up within fifteen minutes of getting the letter, and that was also significant of her wish for secrecy. She could not have known within an hour at what time the letter would come to his hands. The narrow margin of time must have been intended to secure as far as possible that he would have no opportunity of talking to others before she could gain his promise of silence. And even on the phone, she had been quick enough to prevent him giving his name, and the appointment had been made in such a way that anyone who had been listening in would not know within half a square mile where it was that they were arranging to meet.... If she were not avoiding the police, on which point he may be excused a doubt, it was evident that she had some most urgent reason for meeting him in a private manner.

Well, he must wait, with what patience he could, and meanwhile he must return to the magistrates' court, and watch the development of a drama in which it had seemed, a mere week ago, that he was to have been cast for the central part.

He found Inspector Combridge looking out for him as he entered the court. He had no wish either to treat him with lack of confidence or to break his promise to Augusta Garten, whether or not it had been the police she had had in mind. He had prepared himself against such an encounter, and said at once: "Don't ask me now, but tomorrow morning I hope to have something to tell you," and was relieved when the Inspector accepted that assurance, and hurried on, having other urgencies to distract his mind.

CHAPTER THIRTY

Nos. 1 to 20 Vincent Street consisted of a row of adjoining houses which were narrow and high. They had basements, and four floors above, on each of which were two rooms only.

No. 13 was rented by two sisters who, like Mrs. Benson, lived in the basement, and made their living by letting the rooms above. They did the whole work of the house, beside waiting upon their various lodgers, and it is not hard to believe that, as they said, they slept well, and were indifferent to noises during the night.

Of the four floors which they let off, the two rooms at the top were rented by Peter Entwistle.

Those on the next had been occupied by a man named Bigland, and a female companion whom he called his sister, until a few weeks before, when the woman had died, since which date he had been the sole tenant of this floor.

The two rooms on the second floor were rented separately by Miss Vivian Perrin, and Miss Gracie Fortescue, two young ladies who occupied them more or less in common, or as the exigencies of their occupation required. They were frequently out during the night hours, and less disposed to regard the movements of others than concerned that their own should be unobserved. They professed anxiety to assist the police, with whom they preferred to maintain relations as friendly as their occupation allowed, but they said, with apparent frankness, that they were unable to do so on this occasion.

On the ground floor, a single room was rented by Miss Patricia

Welkins, an ancient invalid who shared it with rather numerous cats. She had been an actress in prehistoric days, and was very willing to talk to Inspector Combridge concerning her triumphs and acquaintances during the latter half of the previous century, but she showed less interest in more recent events.

As to people passing in and out during the night, the nuisance was too frequent for the observation or memory of separate instances. On the night of the fourth inst.? No doubt there were. Probably dozens. But she had no detailed recollection whatever.

The opposite room was rented by a registered alien of doubtful character, who was often absent for long periods, of which this had been one. He returned to it four days after the murder, saying that he had been abroad, which his passport confirmed.

All the occupants of the house, except Miss Welkins, were in possession of latchkeys, and went in and out at their own discretion.

Among these people, Inspector Combridge had found in John Bigland the only, and fortunately a valuable and talkative witness. When the court reassembled, Mr. Dunkover put him into the box.

He was a short, thick-bearded man, with a gruff voice, and a grey profusion of unbrushed hair. He suffered from rheumatic troubles, and appeared to walk with difficulty.

He gave his name, and 13 Vincent Street as his address, with an aggressive air, his glance going defiantly right and left over the crowded court, as though challenging contradiction from those who heard.

He said he was a master-plumber by trade. He occupied the two rooms of the third floor of No. 13. There were two attic rooms on the fourth floor over his head.

He explained that he was responsible for two rooms because; one had been occupied until recently by an unmarried sister, who had died about five weeks before. He had been in no haste to give up the room because the furniture and other contents were his. He looked round as he said this as though expecting contradiction, and ready to resent it when it appeared. His attitude stirred a ribald and possibly baseless doubt in some listeners' minds that the lady might have been of a less innocent relationship.

On the night of the fourth he had been awake, suffering from a sharp attack of sciatica. The rooms overhead were occupied by Mr. Entwistle, whom he knew well, and whom he recognized as the man in the dock. He was a left-handed man. He had seen him sign a receipt with his left hand.

He was sure that he would have heard anyone ascend or descend the attic stairs on the night in question. He had, in fact, heard light steps descending at some time before three A.M. He had not doubted that they were those of a woman, and of one who had been anxious not to be overheard. He had supposed that Mr. Entwistle had been entertaining an illicit visitor, and had thought no more about it until Inspector Combridge had interviewed him.

Mr. Huddleston was unable to shake this testimony. The man was aggressively sure that he had not slept. Anyone who had had sciatica would understand that. He had heard no one getting out on to the roof, or entering from it, but it was unreasonable to suppose that he would.

The window which was said to have been used was not in the room over his head, but on the other side.

But the top flight of stairs was uncarpeted. They creaked. They terminated within a foot of his own door. He was fiercely sure that no one could have passed up or down whom he would not have heard.

As to the time when he had heard the steps, it was certainly before three A.M. He knew that because it was before he took some medicine which he had been directed to swallow at that hour. He took the time from the chimes of the nearby church clock.

It was before three. But he could not be more exact. That was because he was telling the truth. Had he been making up lies, he would doubtless have been exact to a minute, or perhaps less.

He left the box truculently, his evidence unshaken.

After this, there was some legal argument, in the course of which Mr. Huddleston submitted that there was no case to answer.

Mr. Garrison showed more hesitation than he would often allow to appear, but finally said that he could not agree. If Mr. Huddleston did not call evidence, he should rule that it was a case for a jury's verdict.

Mr. Huddleston said that in face of that decision he should call his witnesses. He put Peter Entwistle into the box.

CHAPTER THIRTY-ONE

The prisoner entered the witness-box with a blue-coated constable at his side. He took the oath with easy confidence. He gave his name as Peter Musgrave Entwistle. His address as 13 Vincent Street, N.W.1. His occupation, artist.

A hundred curious eyes, fixed intently upon him as he faced the court, observed a man unusually tall, with a long narrow face, in which sandy brows were highly arched over grey vigilant eyes. He had a fresh complexion, and a pleasantly ingratiating manner, better adapted, perhaps, to impress a jury favourably than the more criminally-experienced lawyers by whom he was now surrounded.

Mr. Huddleston's examination was of a pointed and unexpected brevity.

"Mr. Entwistle, you are aware that you are accused of the murder of William Rabone. Did you know this man at all?"

The prisoner smiled slightly, as though at a suggestion that could be easily put aside. "So far as I am aware, I never met nor even heard of him in my life."

"Did you, on the night of the fourth inst., or at any other time, ever enter the attic floor of number seventeen Vincent Street through one of the windows in the roof?"

"Never at any time."

"Were you at home in your rooms at thirteen Vincent Street on the night in question—that of the fourth inst.?"

"No. I was away. I got back about 5:30 A.M."

"Do you know anything whatever of William Rabone's

death?"

"Absolutely nothing more than I have read in the newspapers. I did not hear of it till I read it in the afternoon editions. It didn't enter my head that I could be in any way concerned, he being an utter stranger to me."

"Do you recognize this razor?" The weapon with which the fatal wounds had been inflicted was handed up to the witness.

"So far as I am aware, I have never seen it before."

"Have you, or have you ever had a razor of similar pattern?"

"I have always used a safety-razor. I never in my life possessed one of any other kind."

"Do you swear that you had no part in, nor any knowledge of William Rabone's death, of which you were not even aware until you read the report in the daily press?"

"I do."

"That is all, thank you."

Mr. Huddleston sat down with a smile for Mr. Dunkover which said as plainly as words: "Your witness now! Question him at your own risk," which Mr. Dunkover, uneasily conscious that there was a very probable guile in the method of an examination which left him so much to elucidate, must proceed to do.

"You are," he commenced, "as I have been given to understand, a gentleman of some means?"

"I have a moderate income."

"A considerable capital?"

The witness looked annoyed. The questions were not those which he had been expecting to have to meet. He said: "My uncle left me some money when he died about five years ago."

"How much?"

"About three thousand pounds. But it has increased since then. I have been fortunate in my investments."

"Well, that is what I suggested at first. You are a gentleman of substantial means. Will you tell the court why you occupy rooms which are particularly suitable for getting on to the roof, but which are not otherwise of a particularly desirable character?"

"I am an artist. I find that attic rooms have the best lights."

"Do you recognize it to be a singular coincidence that William Rabone, who was not an artist, had a similar preference for attic rooms?"

"There has been evidence that people visited him during the night."

"But it was not you?"

"It was certainly not I."

"You do not doubt that he was visited in such ways?"

"Why should I? We all heard what the young lady said."

"Nor that she followed the man by whom the murder was surely committed back to the window of your own rooms?"

"How can I tell? I was away. She may have made a mistake in the dark. I should think it would be easy to do."

"And you say that you were away. We will come to that in a moment. You have never used your own windows for such purposes? Never been out on the roofs during the night?"

"Oh yes, I have. Several times."

The reply, and the almost jaunty tone in which it was given, were so unexpected that they checked for a moment even Mr. Dunkover's experienced advocacy, and he was not ready with the following question. He recovered himself quickly, to say: "You are often out on the roofs during the night! May I ask for what purpose you go, and to what address?"

"I didn't say often. I said I had been out several times. I go to No. 11 Vincent Street to visit my wife."

Mr. Dunkover paused again. He had an unquiet conviction that where he had thought that he was leading the witness, Peter Entwistle had really been leading him, and that it would need exceptional caution on his part to avoid falling into further pitfalls. But he could not leave that answer unchallenged and unexplained. He asked: "Does your wife also occupy attic rooms farther along the roof?"

"No. She sometimes stays at No. 11. On those occasions she has a room on the third floor, which another lady underlets to her when she is away."

"And on those occasions you visit her by way of the roof? Can you explain the reasons for this singular method of matrimonial intercourse?"

Mr. Garrison interposed. "I do not wish to embarrass your cross-examination, Mr. Dunkover, but it appears to me that if Entwistle can establish the fact of his having been at No. 11 Vincent Street between midnight and three A.M. of the fifth inst., that is all that he should be asked to do. If he has witnesses of satisfactory character who can testify to that, there must be an end to the present charge."

Mr. Huddleston rose to say that in addition to Mrs. Entwistle's own evidence he had that of Mrs. Musgrave, and of two independent witnesses.

"Mrs. Musgrave?" Mr. Garrison asked.

"I am instructed that Peter Musgrave is my client's true name. He added Entwistle to conform to that of an uncle who brought him up—in fact, the one from whom he inherited the small fortune which he has mentioned."

"Then I will confine myself," Mr. Dunkover began, "to asking—" But the witness interrupted him to say that he would prefer to explain.

He said that he had met and married his wife during a holiday in Cumberland in the previous summer. When on holiday he had always used the name of Musgrave, and that was the only one by which he was known to her.

The marriage was secret, and, as he had no suitable home to which to bring her in London, it had been decided that she should remain with an aunt with whom she had been residing previously, until he could realize his investments, which he was now doing, so that they could then go abroad together.

Some months ago, he heard that a lady at No. 11 Vincent Street wished to let her rooms while she was away on holiday, and he had suggested that his wife should write for them. By a mutually convenient arrangement, she had occupied these rooms on that and subsequent occasions, of which this was the third, and he had visited her without risk of observation, except by the two lodgers on the top floor of No. 11, who let him in, being friends on whose discretion he could rely.

There was little risk of oversight from the attic windows of No. 12, which, unlike most of that row of rather squalid apartment-houses, was occupied by a small family who used its top floor for the storage of lumber only.

Having heard this explanation, Mr. Dunkover decided discreetly to accept it without demur. Its credibility must depend upon the demeanour of the witnesses who were still to come.

There was one other matter on which to test Mr. Entwistle's integrity, or the fertility of his imagination.

"Could you tell the court," Mr. Wendover asked, "how or where you were occupied during the three days preceding that on which you were arrested here?"

"I went away because I didn't like being watched."

"You became conscious that you were under the observation of the police?"

"It wasn't easy to miss."

"But if your conscience were void of offence?"

"Some people might like it. I don't."

"And that is all the explanation you have to give?"

"Well, I'm free to go where I like. I didn't have to throw up a job."

Mr. Garrison gave the witness one of his keenly questioning glances as these questions were asked and answered. A moment before he had said to himself that the man was innocent, and that Inspector Combridge had been barking under the wrong tree.

But it was evident that the questions were unwelcome, and the answers were unconvincing. The witness's irritation was not lessened as Mr. Dunkover went on to ask: "And if, as you say, William Rabone was a stranger to you, and his murder of no concern, will you explain what was the attraction which drew you to this court a week ago, when another man was charged with complicity in the same offence, and in spite of the fact, as you have admitted, that you were hiding from the surveillance of the police?"

"I came because—" He checked the unfinished sentence to say lamely: "A court's a public place, isn't it? I just happened to look in!"

"That is the explanation you have to offer. You just happened to look in!"

With this sarcastic echo of the witness's words, Mr. Dunkover sat down, feeling it to be a better termination than he had expected to reach, and Mr. Huddleston showed his consciousness of an awkward corner by allowing his client to leave the box without endeavouring to remove the impression his answers made. He called Mrs. Jean Musgrave, and a small, fair-haired ineffectual girl, who had been sitting tearfully at the back of the court, came forward and entered the witness-box.

CHAPTER THIRTY-TWO

Mrs. Musgrave, twisting a wet handkerchief in her hands, said that she was the daughter of the late Brigadier-General Seton-Farrimer. She had met Peter Musgrave at Kirkoswald, and married him last July.

She confirmed what he had said concerning her visits to No. 11 Vincent Street.

She did not know that he used the name of Entwistle. She knew nothing of his occupations or manner of life, except that he could paint pictures. She had trusted him absolutely? Yes, of course. Her tone implied that anyone would.

He had been with her on the night of the 4th–5th. There was no possible doubt of that, as it was on the 4th that she had arrived.

"Oh," she said, when questioned on that point, "I was to show this!" She produced the remaining half of a return ticket to Bath, stamped with that date. Her aunt, she explained, was staying at Bath for her health.

She was either telling the simple truth, or was an actress of exceptional merit. It seemed more probable that she was a born fool.

Mr. Dunkover asked no questions, but let her go.

She was followed by two brothers, who gave their names as Edward and Lionel Timmins. They were young men of amiable manners and apparent honesty. Edward was a metal engraver, Lionel a compositor. They said that they had known Mr. Entwistle since they had attended classes at which he taught in a Technical School, some years before. He had shown a kindly interest in their future welfare, and had got Edward his present job.

They had opened their skylight window to let him in at about midnight on the night of the 4th, to which point their evidence was identical. It was true that only Edward had seen him leave at about five-thirty on the following morning, but this difference rather increased than diminished the value of their testimony, by the impression of veracity which it gave.

Mr. Dunkover, making a hopeless effort, suggested that they might have been mistaken about the date, and they gave confirmatory particulars which left their evidence even more firmly established than it had been previously.

Mr. Huddleston, rising confidently, asked for the discharge of his client, "for whose arrest," he said boldly, "I suggest that the police never had any reasonably sufficient ground."

Mr. Garrison asked Mr. Dunkover what he had to say in opposition to that application.

Mr. Dunkover, seeing no remaining possibility but to conduct a dignified retreat with such of the honours of war as might still be his, made a short and forcible speech, in which he dwelt upon the strength of Miss Weston's evidence, and the confirmation it received from that of John Bigland, who had heard her steps—and no others—descending during the night.

It was, he argued, beyond reasonable doubt that she had followed the murderer to Peter Entwistle's window, and seen him enter. Was it not the natural presumption that the man was the occupant of the rooms to which he retreated after the crime was committed? If he were a stranger, how did he know that he could find an asylum there? Did he know that Peter was absent? Had he his permission to use his rooms?

He reminded the magistrate that, according to Miss Weston's testimony, it was not the first time that a man had visited William Rabone during the night, and retired through Peter Entwistle's window.

If it were not Peter himself, then it was reasonably certain that Peter must know who it was. Why did he not assist the police? Would he be likely to keep silent, and risk conviction, to protect another man—and one who had been guilty of a murder which must be repellent to all decent minds?

Then there was the fact that Peter was a left-handed man. Surely a most unlikely coincidence that he and the murderer who made midnight use of his rooms should both have this somewhat unusual peculiarity!

Finally, there was the fact that he had gone into hiding when he became suspicious that his movements were under the observation of the police. Was that the act of an innocent man, who, as he had sworn, had no idea that he could be held to have had any connection with the crime? And what, except a knowledge of his own guilt, could have been the force which had drawn him to that court when another man had stood in the dock, charged with the same offence?

It was a rearguard action, in which he was not discredited. But it was common realization among the legal gentlemen who surrounded him that his cause was lost.

Mr. Garrison, silently reviewing the evidence of the police witnesses, who had been so much less numerous than their names (he had thought of a good joke on that, which he had restrained with difficulty, but he made it a rule—in which he showed better manners than some High Court judges—that he would never jest when a prisoner stood before him on the capital charge), observed that there was only that of Miss Weston, supported in one detail by John Bigland, which threw direct suspicion upon the accused, and she was unable to identify the man she had followed.

As it stood, it was a case of suspicion rather than proof, and with the alibi in the other scale—! He could not commit a prisoner for trial with the certainty in his own mind that no jury would convict. He said: "I have decided that the evidence is not sufficient to justify a committal. The prisoner will be discharged."

He saw the three heads of Mr. Huddleston, K.C., Mr.

Augustus Pippin, and Mr. Richard Middleton, Junior, very closely together. He overheard words from which he judged correctly that they were debating whether they should have the temerity to ask for costs against the police. He saved them the trouble of further words by saying: "I should add that it was a case in which I consider the police were fully justified in the arrest they made. I am satisfied that Peter Entwistle could assist the police, if he were of a mind to do so, and that the position in which he found himself was the result of his own conduct, which was not such as should be expected from a good citizen, or an entirely innocent man."

Inspector Combridge must take what comfort he could from this magisterial exculpation. It did not alter the fact that he had put two men successively into the dock, and that the murderer was still unfound.

Could it be possible that Miss Weston's tale, if it were not entirely concocted, yet withheld some essential facts, perhaps out of sympathy with the murderer, even if she had not shared or connived in the crime?

As he sat in court during that last hour in which he had seen beyond doubt how the case would end, he had gone minutely over Francis Hammerton's evidence, to observe, from that angle, how far it corroborated her own, and at what point he must regard her account of the night's events as being unsupported by any independent testimony.

Might she not have committed the crime herself, urged by the hatred which she had no care to conceal, and seeing Rabone to be contemptuous of being caught in the meshes of the criminal law, as she had hoped that, by her instrumentality, he was destined to be?

Her account of the offer he had made to her that evening, the long discussion that followed, her pretence of agreement, the quarrel on the upper floor—all of them might be no more than inventions of her own mind. Only one man could have denied her tale, and he was dead, by whatever hand.

It might be accepted as facts that, at some time before the

murder, she had lain down on her bed, but had not taken off her clothes, and that she had left her room by the window within a few minutes of Rabone's death.

But why should he not have died by her own hand, and she fled, to gain the street by means of the other house, and then appear next day with this plausible, invented tale?

Might she not have known that Entwistle would be away, and that she could enter No. 11, and descend into the street, with little fear that anyone would obstruct her way?

Bigland's testimony, so far as it went, was consistent with such an interpretation of the crime. A woman's feet—and no more.

What was there against it?

In the first place, the murder appeared lo be the work of a tall, left-handed man. (How exactly Entwistle fitted that part! How exasperating that alibi was!) In the second, the windows in *both* rooms had been open.

That was a smaller point, but it supported the first, and inclined him to think that the crime was the work of another hand, though she might have stood by, or assisted the murderer to escape unseen.

He decided that she knew more than she had disclosed, and that a talk with Mr. Banks would be useful. And, better still, there was Sir Reginald Crowe. Perhaps their combined influences might persuade her to a fuller frankness.

As he left the court with these thoughts in his mind, alternating with visions of himself reduced, for incompetence, to the ignominy of a uniformed beat, he observed Francis Hammerton in the corridor. Francis, who had been waiting for him, came up to ask: "I wonder whether you would do me a favour for a few hours?"

"Hadn't you got something to tell me when I saw you this morning?"

"No. I said I hoped to have something tomorrow."

"About Rabone, or your own case?"

"I don't know yet. It may be nothing. It's just a chance. I

want to ask you to promise me that I shan't be followed about tonight."

"You mean you've heard from Miss Garten?"

"I didn't say so. I only say I don't want to be followed about tonight, as I know I am; and if you'll do that for me, I'll find out anything I can about the Rabone murder."

Inspector Combridge may be excused some hesitation in his reply.

"I don't know," he said, "whether you've thought that you may be safer wherever you're meaning to go—I'm not asking you where it is—if one of our men has you in sight?"

"I'll risk that. I've got so much at stake that."

"Yes. I suppose you have. Well, it's a deal. I'll trust you not to let Sir Reginald down. You know you mean two thousand to him."

"You'll see me at Scotland Yard at 10:30 tomorrow morning, if I'm alive."

"Very well. I'll call Beddoes off."

He watched Francis as he disappeared rapidly up Alderman Street. "I wonder," he asked himself, "whether I'm being a bigger fool than before?" Suppose they had all been in it together? He imagined a little supper of celebration. Peter Entwistle in the chair, with Mary Weston and Francis on either hand, and perhaps the two Timmins brothers farther away, and the tearful Jean at the foot of the table. Obviously Francis would not wish the police to observe him on such an occasion!

"I wonder," he thought again, "whether it's just ordinary imbecility that's got me, or premature senile decay?"

CHAPTER THIRTY-THREE

When Francis Hammerton left Inspector Combridge, he had three hours to waste before the time of his appointment in Deal Street, but he was too restless to return to his own room, or he would have got the letter which afterwards fell into the Inspector's hands, and many things might have happened differently.

He spent an hour in a tea-shop, and then wandered up and down Piccadilly in a state of increasing anxiety as to what, if anything, would be the result of his interview with Augusta Garten.

He remembered that her promise had not been unconditional, a point which had not previously impressed his mind as much as, perhaps, it should. But, as the hour approached, the doubt grew, and patience became proportionately difficult.

Yet he had sufficient sense not to attempt to keep the appointment before the time she had fixed, and to see that, as she had made so strict a condition of secrecy, there would be no wisdom in walking up and down outside the restaurant for the hour before he was due to enter. He kept away from the immediate neighbourhood of Deal Street until a few minutes to seven, and then walked quickly to it, and through the ground-floor restaurant without haste, but as one who knows where he is going, and in a manner least likely to draw the attention of others upon himself.

As he passed through he observed, with his eyes rather than his mind, two men who occupied a seat by the door, whose faces were vaguely familiar, but he was too preoccupied by the doubt of whether he might be going up to find no more than an empty room to give attention to them.

What had she said? "I may be there, or I mayn't. It depends." Those, if his memory did not fail, were her exact words. There was no promise in them.

But by now he was up the narrow twisting stairs, and saw that it was at least sure that he was not approaching an unoccupied room, for a waiter was in the act of leaving the second door on the right, with an empty tray in his hand.

He went up to the door, knocked, and entered.

Augusta Garten was on a couch against the farther wall, her blonde head lying back, a half-smoked cigarette between carmined lips, and her eyes fixed on the ceiling in frowning thought.

Her glance turned lazily toward him, and then changed to a look of terror.

"Why," she said in a tone of equal anger and fear, "did you come, when I told you not? You must go at once! I'm in danger enough through you, without this."

But Francis was in no mood to retreat from an angry word, even had he understood her reproach.

"I don't know what you mean," he said. "You told me to come."

"Didn't you get my letter?"

"Yes. You know I did. That was why I rang you up this morning."

"Don't waste time! I mean the second one. But don't stay talking now. You must go."

"It doesn't seem to be a very dangerous place." He looked round the quiet, comfortable room, in the centre of which a table was laid for three, with a smile which declined to respond to the note of panic in her voice.

"Don't be an utter fool!" she said sharply. "It isn't only danger for you. I've been suspected ever since you advertised to half London that you were looking everywhere for me." Her words came rapidly, as though talking against time, as she added: "Tell

Inspector Combridge to arrest me tonight at 14 Linfield Street. When I'm safe, I'll tell him all that he wants to know.

"You've seen me in the street and followed me here, and I've told you to clear out. I don't want to see you again as long as I live."

As she spoke these last words, there was a sound of voices in the corridor, as a waiter directed someone to the room he required. Her voice sank, as she added hurriedly: "You've done it now! Don't believe anything I say, or anyone else. And *don't let yourself be persuaded to stay....*" She raised her voice to add: "I've told you I don't want to see you again as long as I live, and you might have the decency to leave a room where no one asked you to come."

At the same moment, the door opened, and Mr. Jesse Banks entered the room.

Francis looked at him in a natural surprise, but had sufficient presence of mind not to show that he knew him for whom he was. He had, in fact, only seen him casually in court, when he had been pointed out to him as Miss Weston's employer. Now he wondered, in one instant of doubt, whether Augusta Garten could know him, or in what name or guise he might have penetrated into the counsels of the gang to whom she belonged.

He did not think it singular that he had not heard before that the enquiry agent was so closely upon their track, for it was only from Mr. Jellipot that he received any real confidence. Inspector Combridge might doubt whether he were suffering from imbecility or senile decay, but he would have diagnosed his condition as beyond question or remedy had he become confidential with the convict whose innocence was still one of the uncertain problems that vexed his mind.

Actually, if he would not have been as surprised as Francis Hammerton to see Mr. Banks enter that room, it was only because he was aware of the jealousy which divides the official from the private investigator. Mr. Banks was instructed by the London & Northern Bank. It was to them that his loyalty was due, and to whom his first report should be made. He would be very unlikely to inform Inspector Combridge of the details of what he did, or of the line of enquiry on which he was engaged until its result should appear.

Mr. Banks might not suppose himself to be known to Francis, but he showed at once that Francis was known to him.

"I was not aware," he said smoothly, "that you would have been a visitor here. Mr. Vaughan, is it not?"

"Mr. Vaughan," Augusta replied, "has come uninvited into my private room, and I have just told him to clear out."

"Oh," Mr. Banks replied, "but I don't see why you should take that line. Mr. Vaughan's in an awkward mess. We ought to give him any help that we can. Now he's here, you might ask him to stay."

The words were no more than a request, but the tone was that of one who assumed that his wishes would be obeyed.

"Of course," Augusta replied, "he can stay if you wish."

"I'll ring for another place to be laid."

Francis hesitated. She had warned him that it would be dangerous for him to remain: that he was to disregard anything that anyone, including herself, might say. She had told him to ask Inspector Combridge to find some pretext for her arrest, so that, he must presume, she could betray those who had ceased to trust her, within the safety of prison walls. She was to be found that night at 14 Pinfold Street? No, it was not that. Linford Street? That seemed nearer, but he did not think it was right. There are so many streets in London! It would be useless to give the Inspector an uncertain name.... Probably in a few minutes it would come back to his mind.

In the meantime, he would not go. Everything might depend upon getting that name correctly. It was maddening to think that it could so quickly have left his mind! But it had all been so hurriedly said.... And the risk might be much less than Miss Garten feared, not knowing Mr. Banks for the friend of order and law.... And Mr. Banks had made it clear that he wished him to stay. He might even be relying upon him for some form of support.... He would remain, at the least, until he had recollected that name. Linford—Linton—it had been something like that. Or perhaps he would have an opportunity of asking Augusta again.

These were the thoughts of the fifteen seconds while Augusta rose lazily from the couch, and moved to the bell, and his reply paused. Then he said:

"I don't want to intrude, but if you're sure that I shan't be in the way?"

If Miss Garten wished him to go she gave no sign. She said: "Of course, we can't let you go at this hour without some dinner. I'm sorry I lost my temper, but I'm frightened of everything since you and Tony got caught.... Colonel Driver ought to be here any minute now. You've met him before," And as she spoke the last member of the little party, a rather heavily-built, middle-aged man, of almost too pronounced a military aspect, entered the room.

CHAPTER THIRTY-FOUR

The meal commenced quietly. Under an outward suavity, it might be that each of the four who sat round the small square table was watchful, suspicious, anxious for others to show their hands, as they were careful to hide their own.

Colonel Driver looked alternately at Francis and Mr. Banks, as though seeking the answer to a riddle that he was too cautious to ask. Mr. Banks may have intended to give that answer when he said: "I expect Mr. Vaughan feels a bit sore over the way things went. But he's done the right thing in looking us up." He spoke directly to Francis as he concluded: "You might tell us how matters stand, and we'll put our heads together to see what we can do."

Augusta added: "We've heard you got bail, and that there's an appeal coming on, but we've no idea how you managed that, or how you got mixed up in the Rabone murder. You must have a lot to tell us, and I'm just dying to hear."

Francis was not slow to take a lead which came from two whom he had reason to think his friends, even though they might each suppose themselves to be the only one there. He saw that, if he could obtain an admission that he had been Tony Welch's dupe, with Mr. Banks for witness, would have the additional evidence upon which Mr. Jellipot had insisted as the only legal weapon that would be sufficient to set him free.

He replied by narrating his experiences from the moment when he had walked out of the detention room at the Central Criminal Court, and stating as frankly as though he had been talking to Augusta Garten alone, the errand on which he came. He was silent only concerning his promise to Inspector Combridge that he would seek also for information bearing on the Rabone murder, judging that he would be more likely to learn anything in that company if it were not suspected that he would pass it on to the police.

He did this with few interruptions, for Mr. Banks, having given his cue, had relapsed into his habitual silence, and only Colonel Driver asked an occasional question with the veneer of good-humoured geniality which hid, at least to casual or unpractised eyes, the hard lines of cruelty and sensuality into which his face would settle at unguarded times.

If, as Francis thought, Mr. Banks had deliberately led the conversation in such a way that he might become a witness to the admission that he had been an innocent dupe rather than an active participant in the conspiracy for which he had been convicted, the result must have been all that either of them desired.

Colonel Driver did not question the fact. He admitted that it was natural that Francis should feel a grievance when he had found himself in the dock on a criminal charge. But that had not been an anticipated result. The more probable termination of the incident would have been that he would have received a substantial sum of money as part of the profit of the coup in which he had taken a useful though unconscious part. After that, he might have been willing to engage in other adventures in a more deliberate manner.

The Colonel mentioned that Miss Garten had been an unconscious decoy in her first introduction to the methods of livelihood to which she was now accustomed.

Augusta confirmed that she had been used, during a voyage to the Far East, to infatuate a youth of more money than brains, while he was relieved at the card-table of that which, it was considered, might be in much better hands.

"But," she said, "I didn't mind when I knew. He was only a soppy fool."

They had given her a hundred pounds, which had been wealth to her at the time, and she had remained in their company with an understanding, unspoken but no less clearly agreed, that she was available for similar use when the next occasion should come.

Francis, remembering his own experience, saw that her rôle had not changed, nor her efficiency failed, though she might not have the same innocency of allure which had made her an invaluable acquisition to the gang ten years before.

He saw that, indirectly, but as certainly as the invitation had been given to her, it was being extended to him.

It was a temptation which he could resist without difficulty, and even to feign acceptance would have seemed dangerous with Mr. Banks silently listening.

Considering that, and the fact that Augusta Garten had asked to be arrested so that she could betray her associates, he was explicit in making it clear that he sought no more than his own vindication, and had no desire for further experience of the precarious profits of crime.

He did not expect that the Colonel would volunteer to assist him on such conditions. But he was indifferent on that point, thinking that the pseudo-military gentleman was unconsciously doing all that his necessity required, as he talked, and Mr. Banks silently listened.

But Colonel Driver seemed willing even to contemplate giving him the help he needed.

"We mustn't let you go back to quod," he said genially. "We'll have to get you a witness that the old fossils will hear. The question is who's going to be the goat. Well, you must leave that to me."

Understanding that it was His Majesty's Judges of the Court of Appeal to whom the Colonel alluded in that disrespectful manner, Francis felt that he was being met better than he had had reason to hope. He even began to doubt whether he were not acting with rather contemptible treachery in leading Colonel Driver to expose himself to the doubtless retentive memory of the silent Banks. But he reflected reasonably that he had been no party to the introduction of the enquiry agent to the inner councils of Augusta's associates. The dinner certainly had not been arranged by him.

Having come to that point of understanding and promise, the Colonel led the conversation in other ways, and Mr. Banks, whose silence had allowed him to consume an excellent meal, rose, as one who had completed the purpose for which he came.

He said to Colonel Driver: "You'll know what to do tonight," to which he received a cheerfully affirmative reply. He said good night casually to Augusta, and politely to Francis, whom he continued to address as Mr. Vaughan.

Francis noticed that no one had addressed Mr. Banks by name, and was sufficiently cautious to avoid it himself. He was not outwardly disguised, which is a clumsy expedient at the best, but who knew what separate personality he might not have assumed, to enable him to gain the confidence of these wary and unscrupulous criminals?

Francis thought that Augusta Garten became paler after he left, that she had more difficulty in maintaining an outward calmness or gaiety than she had shown previously. He felt in better spirits himself. Even if the Colonel were no better than a false friend, even if Augusta Garten, and perhaps he himself, were in peril, the nature of which he could only vaguely guess, he supposed that Mr. Banks would not leave them unwatched. Probably—almost certainly—Augusta was unaware of the identity or real character of the man who had left the room.

CHAPTER THIRTY-FIVE

When Mr. Banks left, Francis had also begun to think of leaving. He had got all for which he had hoped, it might even be said twice over, if Colonel Driver's half-promise should prove to be of genuine worth. For there would be the testimony of Mr. Banks, surely sufficient in itself, even should the Colonel fail to produce the "goat" whose evidence might be difficult to frame in a convincing manner without self-implication, or betrayal of members of the gang other than Tony Welch who had not yet fallen into the hands of a hostile law.

Yet he hesitated, being delayed by memory of his promise to Inspector Combridge that he would endeavour to obtain information concerning the Rabone murder, which he had as yet made no effort to fulfil; and by a faint hope that the Colonel might offer to leave before him, and so give the opportunity he sought to ask Augusta for the name of the street which still eluded his memory.

But as he watched for an opportunity of leading the conversation toward the Vincent Street tragedy, he had a sudden instinctive fear of what the consequence to himself might be, if there should come even a doubt into Colonel Driver's mind of the reason for which he asked. The end of William Rabone was unpleasantly suggestive of the payment which traitors earned.

And from that thought there came, by natural sequence, a recollection of the hurried warning that Augusta Garten had given before the two men had entered the room. He was to believe nothing that was said—nothing, even by herself. And how evident, how real had been the fear that she had expressed! How drastic the course which she had proposed for her own security!

Something of his satisfaction in Colonel Driver's attitude, something of the sense of security which he had derived from the presence of Mr. Banks, left him with this memory, and it was with a resolution that he would not longer delay his going that he returned his wandering attention to the conversation which the Colonel was sustaining, with the suavity that his actual rather than his expressed profession required.

He was talking now of an exploit of aviation which had been the subject of headlines in the afternoon papers. Did Mr. Vaughan take an interest in such matters? Had he perhaps some knowledge of flying himself? There were so many of the younger generation who were drawn to the adventure of the air, who might even hold pilots' certificates unguessed by any but their most intimate friends.

Francis agreed that there were, but admitted that he was not one. Even as a passenger, he had never flown. He had a dread of crashing. It was not so much the danger of death as an abstract fear, as that of death by burning, if a plane should fall in flames, as so many did. He had a special horror of fire as an agent of violent death.

Colonel Driver said politely that there were many such. "There's Augusta here," he went on, "who's got better nerves than most women or men either, but we couldn't get her to fly from Berlin, even though she knew she ran a bigger risk of five years in a German jail every minute that she delayed."

"It wasn't really that," Augusta said, rather as one who was making conversation than as having any real interest in the subject, "I thought it was running more risk, all trying to get off together like that. It seemed like walking into a trap, where we'd be easy to catch.... I saw I was wrong afterwards, when you all got through safely, and I'd still got to wriggle out."

The Colonel received this explanation with a polite incredulity. He said he recalled the terror she had expressed at the time, but he understood her reluctance to admit to so extreme a fear of that which many women of weaker nerves could accept without tremors.

Augusta made no reply, letting the subject drop, and Francis, seeing that the Colonel showed no disposition to leave, said that he must be going.

Colonel Driver looked up at that. He said: "So we will. We will all go.... Here is something that I should like you to see."

He pulled out an automatic, which he laid on the table before him, but with his hand still upon it.

"You are familiar with modern firearms? Not particularly? Then you may not know that this is an automatic pistol, and this is a silencer which is fixed upon it. Its use would be that, if I should shoot you both, there would be no noise that would penetrate through that rather solid door. I could walk out, and be far away before any suspicion would be aroused."

Francis heard the menace in the quiet voice. He realized that the Colonel had a cruel enjoyment in the fear that his words must cause, that it would be with a keener joy that he would turn the deadly weapon upon them, and see their bodies wilt and fall as the continuous stream of bullets poured from no more than the table's breadth.

He had an instant's thought of wonder that the deadly crisis, as he recognized it to be, did not disturb his mind from what seemed an unnatural coolness, a clarity that made a leisured minute of that instant of time. He was on the point of resolving to push the table, by a sudden motion, toward the Colonel, trusting to upset him and his chair with a violence which might separate the pistol from his hand, or enable it to be seized before he could recover himself for its use, but was deterred by the sound of Miss Garten's voice, controlled to a more casual level than was consistent with the evidence of her bloodless face.

"Of course you could, but for the fact that people don't shoot each other for no reason at all."

"No?" the Colonel answered harshly. "But the greatest reason of all is a rather different matter."

"Which you know quite well," she answered boldly, "you haven't got.... As well," she added, "as I know that you won't be fool enough to do what you'd like to frighten us into thinking you will."

He looked at her with a cruel smile as he answered: "And if you're so sure, perhaps you'll tell me why."

"Because, if you'd meant to do it at all, you'd have done it without talking."

His manner altered as he replied: "You're right, Augusta, as you mostly are. I've always said you're no fool. Though I don't say what I should be if I were to trust you again. But I'll tell you both that I shan't injure a hair of your heads if you have the sense to come quietly with me to where we can talk these matters over better than we can here."

"Yes," she answered for both, "we'll do that," and Francis saw that, for the moment, they had passed the crisis of life and death, and his knee relaxed from its pressure upon the table, and his eyes from their unwinking watch of Colonel Driver's hand.

The next moment, as though his demonstration of power should be sufficient without further effort, the Colonel rose easily. He dropped the pistol back into the side-pocket from which it came, and walked over to the bell, which he pressed, with the remark: "It's the rule here that a waiter doesn't come to these rooms after nine P.M. unless he's sure that he's wanted to show his face. The women, like—don't they, Augusta?—to know that they're sure of that."

His back was turned for the instant that he was pressing the bell, and the eyes of his captives met in a question to which Francis thought that Augusta answered with a warning of caution, as though she would not have him hasten an event in which time might lessen the peril in which they stood.

The Colonel came back to the table. He sat down, as with a recovered urbanity. He asked, as the waiter entered: "Do you mind telling me how you found your way here tonight?— It's the bill, Alphonso, I want. We're just going now."

Francis remembered the warning that Augusta had given,

which had prepared his mind for the needed lie.

"I saw Miss Garten as I was coming up Deal Street. I've been looking for her ever since Friday. I thought if she couldn't help me herself, she'd tell me which of you I ought to ask. So when I saw her come here I followed her in."

"Which way was she coming when you saw her? Up the street or down?"

"She was crossing over."

The Colonel accepted this. Francis thought he half-believed. It suggested a possibility that Augusta might succeed in asserting her own innocence, with his help, even though his own danger might not be less. And then there was the fact that Mr. Banks knew how he had left them, and might guess something of the peril in which they were. Probably it was best to go slowly, to wait events. But, of course, if a chance should come—

The bill was paid now, and the waiter gone. The Colonel rose. He said to Augusta: "We'll go now. I've got Morton's car here. We'll go there, and talk it over with him."

Francis could not remember who Morton was, but he thought the girl looked relieved, as though there were hope in the suggestion. It made him more disposed to go quietly with them, and yet, he wondered, how could Colonel Driver secure that they would not leave him when they were once clear of the restaurant doors? Would he try to shoot them both in the street? If he set any value on his own life, it did not seem a likely thing to attempt.

They went down the narrow stairs, the Colonel leading the way, and came into the restaurant. It was nearly empty now, the diners having left, and the after-theatre crowd not begun to arrive, but the two men whom Francis had noticed when he came in were still seated by the door.

They rose at the Colonel's appearance, and came up the room. Seeing that they were doing this, he turned, and led the way out at a side-door which opened to a narrow passage, leading to one of those cul-de-sacs which are numerous among the side streets between Park Lane and Charing Cross Road.

The Colonel went first, followed by Augusta and Francis, the two men close at his rear. The cul-de-sac, so far as the ill-lit darkness showed, was empty except for the waiting car.

Colonel Driver said nothing to the chauffeur, who must have had his orders before. He said to Augusta: "You'd better go in the front."

Francis found himself beside the Colonel on the rear seat.

The two men turned away. The car was soon running smoothly and swiftly westward along the Bayswater Road.

CHAPTER THIRTY-SIX

"The question now is whether William Rabone were engaged in a conspiracy to defraud the bank, as I am much inclined to believe, and was murdered by associates whom he was proposing to betray for his own security, or whether he were a faithful servant to us, and lost his life through his zeal in tracing the authors of the frauds from which we were suffering.

"It is a question to which I am resolved that the answer shall be discovered, and, to secure this end, I am prepared to offer a reward of two thousand pounds for information which will lead to the conviction of the criminal."

"You think," Mr. Jellipot said doubtfully, when Sir Reginald had made this announcement, "that, if you discover the murderer, you will learn the motive of the crime?"

They were in Sir Reginald's office, where he had also invited Mr. Banks and Inspector Combridge to meet him at noon on the day following Peter Entwistle's release, to take counsel together.

The time was now 12:15, for Inspector Combridge, who was usually a punctual man, had been ten minutes late, and Sir Reginald had deferred this announcement till he arrived.

"Yes," Sir Reginald replied, "I think when we know that, we shall soon know enough to get at the rest."

Mr. Banks, a man of few words, nodded his agreement with this opinion.

Inspector Combridge might have said the same, but he had something else on his mind.

"Two thousand pounds is a big sum. It ought to make someone

squeal. But I'm sorry to say that's just the amount you may have to lose in another way, though I hope I'm wrong."

He had no need to be more explicit before Sir Reginald had guessed his meaning, and repudiated the suggestion which it conveyed.

"You mean Hammerton's jumped his bail? You won't make me believe that. If I couldn't tell when a man's crooked, or when he's straight, I shouldn't be sitting here now. What makes you think that?"

Inspector Combridge was in a chastened mood. A Chief Inspector who has developed a habit of arresting innocent men cannot reasonably object to being charged with deficient judgement of criminal character. It did not occur to him to retort that, if Sir Reginald Crowe were so excellent a judge of the probity of others, it was strange that he should have failed to detect the authors of the frauds from which his bank had suffered so severely and over such a prolonged period, or that he should still have the character of William Rabone in doubt. He only said: "I'm not saying he's jumped his bail. But he's disappeared, and that comes to the same thing, if we can't give an explanation to please the court in about ten days from now.

"You'll say it's my fault, for he asked me to let him go somewhere last night without being watched, and I was fool enough to agree.

"He said I could trust him to report at ten-thirty this morning, if he were still alive, and he hoped to have got some information which I should be glad to have.

"When I'd waited till 11:30, and he hadn't come, I began to think he'd bolted, and to wonder whether he weren't the murderer after all, and had bluffed us with a tale that Miss Weston agreed to support—if you think it out, you'll see how everything fits in. Whatever had happened, I thought I'd better not break my appointment here, but I wanted to learn as much as I could first, so I drove round to the address he'd given us, and found that he hadn't been in since yesterday morning, which looks bad.

"But there was a letter addressed to him on the hall-table,

which I took the liberty of opening. It appears to have been posted in the West Central District yesterday morning, and delivered during the afternoon. There isn't much of it, but you may think it suggests an explanation of a different kind."

As he spoke, he pulled out a mauve envelope, from which he abstracted a single sheet of paper of the same colour. In a large, bold, probably feminine handwriting, hastily scrawled, were the two words: "Don't come."

"It looks to me," Sir Reginald said, "like a case of foul play."

"That's what I'm inclined to think. As a matter of fact, I warned him of the risk he ran, but he said he didn't care, having so much at stake. I thought at the time that he was straight, and meant what he said. I don't say he wasn't now. But you can take this letter two ways. It might be a warning, or it might be no more than a change of plan."

"Beyond the postmark, it gives you no clue?"

"Only that it was posted without blotting, and before the ink had had time to dry." He showed the blurred address as he spoke. "But you can read that in more ways than one. It might be done in a hurry, to be unobserved, or merely to catch a post that was due out."

"You've no idea where he was going?"

"Not the least, except that it was almost certainly somewhere in London, as he expected to be able to report to me first thing this morning, and this letter supports that probability."

Mr. Banks interrupted to ask: "May I see the letter, Inspector?"

He took it, and handed it back after what seemed no more than a casual glance. He asked: "No idea whose writing it is?"

"No, I wish I had."

Mr. Banks said nothing more, appearing to lose interest in the subject, but it was a conclusion that anyone who knew him would be slow to draw.

Sir Reginald asked: "You won't lose any time in starting a search?"

"There'll be every available man on it at the present moment.

I telephoned the Yard as soon as I got this letter, and learnt that he hadn't got back to his room last night."

Sir Reginald turned to the lawyer to ask: "I suppose he didn't tell you anything, Jellipot?"

"No, I can't say that he did." But in spite of this negative reply, Mr. Jellipot looked mildly satisfied. He added: "I'm sorry about Hammerton, but I daresay he'll come through all right. I don't think it ought to be long before we see everything cleared up now."

Mr. Banks permitted himself to look slightly surprised. "I wonder," he asked, "what makes you feel sure of that?"

"Well," Mr. Jellipot said, "there are two things. Two thousand pounds is a large sum. If Sir Reginald offers that, it ought to make somebody talk. And then it looks as though someone's afraid of the enquiries that Hammerton was trying to make. That's a good sign, and it's better still if they haven't the nerve to lie low and do nothing. If they try any violence against Hammerton, it's a likely chance that they put themselves into our hands."

Mr. Banks said that it sounded simple when Mr. Jellipot put it like that. There was sarcasm in his voice.

Mr. Jellipot replied mildly that he didn't mean that it was a problem which he would he equal to solving. It was not in his line. He relied for that upon the expert gentlemen to whom he was speaking now.

Sir Reginald, seeing some lack of geniality in these exchanges between gentlemen on whose help he relied, interposed to ask the inspector if he were satisfied with the strength of the alibi that Entwistle had set up.

He replied that he had already given instructions for it to be examined with the thoroughness that the case required. The characters and antecedents, even the identity of the witnesses, would not be accepted without verification. Mrs. Musgrave had been followed from the moment she left the court.

But he was more disposed, for the moment, to consider whether more could not be obtained from Miss Weston than she had yet told. He would ask both Sir Reginald, as having recommended her to the opportunity she had sought, and Mr. Banks, as her employer, to use all their influence for a fuller disclosure of the night's events than she had yet made.

Sir Reginald said that he would be pleased to have a talk with her, but he was strongly disposed to think that she had told the truth already.

Mr. Banks did not decline, but showed no interest in the proposal. He reverted to the question of Peter Entwistle's innocence, concerning which he showed a sustained scepticism. Sir Reginald remembered that he had influenced the inspector previously toward Peter's arrest. Inspector Combridge may have remembered it also, and without gratitude.

Mr. Banks suggested that a reward, however large, could not discover a non-existent criminal. He implied that when they turned their eyes away from Peter Entwistle, they were losing time, and offering a reward which no one could be in a position to claim.

He brought out the point that while a man cannot, by English law, be tried twice for the same offence, Peter Entwistle had not gained this immunity, as the magistrate had declined to commit him, and, technically, he had not been tried at all.

Inspector Combridge admitted this, but without interest. He returned to the subject of Mary Weston.

Sir Reginald saw that Mr. Banks appeared to be irritating the Inspector, as he had done Mr. Jellipot previously. He reflected that, when things are not going well, good humour is not easy to maintain, even among those who are normally friends.

Mr. Banks said he had another appointment, and went.

Inspector Combridge, who was anxious to take personal direction of the search for Francis Hammerton, promptly followed.

Sir Reginald asked Mr. Jellipot to remain for a few minutes, as he had other business requiring the lawyer's attention.

Having dealt with this, he returned to the subject of William Rabone's murder.

"I don't suppose," he said, "that Miss Weston really knows more than she has told us already, and I've got a board meeting on this afternoon, and more other business than I know how to get through. But I'll arrange, if I can get hold of her, that she shall call at your office this afternoon; and if there's more to be learned, there's no one who'll get it out of her better than you.

"I think she has a rather friendly feeling for young Hammerton, and if you tell her he's in jeopardy, as I'm afraid he is, it mayn't do any harm."

Mr. Jellipot, without showing much confidence in this line of enquiry, said that he would do what he could.

CHAPTER THIRTY-SEVEN

It was slightly before four o'clock that afternoon when Miss Weston called at Mr. Jellipot's office. She was shown in at once, and the lawyer greeted her cordially.

"It was good of you," he said, "to come so promptly. Sir Reginald thought that something might be gained if we went over all that happened on the night of the murder together." He added doubtfully: "I don't know that we shall. You seemed to me to give your account very clearly, and to have acted with unusual courage and self-control.... Besides, I expect Mr. Banks has been over the same ground with you since lunch, and you're about sick of the whole subject."

"Yes, I am rather," Miss Weston answered. She had, in fact, lost interest in the uncongenial occupation of crime-detection with the death of the man in whose evil-doing she was directly concerned. She would have left the employment of the Texall Agency at once, had not Mr. Banks insisted that he was entitled to a month's notice, which she could not deny, and kept her sitting in his offices with little to occupy her time, and for no reason that she could see, except that he must wish to keep her in sight until the cause and responsibility of the Rabone murder had been resolved.

But Mr. Jellipot had the voice of a friend, and she answered frankly: "I can't say that Mr. Banks has been bothering me. I came over because Sir Reginald Crowe telephoned, and asked me to do so. He said he'd take the responsibility of my leaving the office. So I waited for some time, but Mr. Banks hasn't been in since lunch, and I thought I'd better come.... I don't really think I can help you at all.... I know Mr. Banks thinks it was Peter Entwistle, and it does seem likely in a good many ways. He's done all he could to get me to say that the man I saw was like him, but I can't honestly. Really, I didn't see him at all, apart from one leg."

"And there was nothing that you could recognize in that?"

"No, there wasn't. I looked at Peter Entwistle's legs particularly. They seemed different to me, but of course he would have changed what he wore."

"So he would. It is more than probable that there would have been blood on either the trousers or boots, especially as the murderer moved about the room in the dark after committing the crime. It is not certain—the fact that the assault was from behind makes it possible that he may have avoided bloodstains entirely if he acted with sufficient care—but it is a very probable thing. Did you notice nothing whatever by which identification would be possible?"

"No. I don't think I could. You must remember it was only a moment's glimpse, as I switched on the light, and the leg was drawn over the window-sill."

She paused, as though on the verge of something she hesitated or feared to say, and Mr. Jellipot waited in a discreet silence that tempted her to go on.

"It just shows," she said at last, "how unreliable such identifications can be, and I only mention it for that reason. but the only time I've seen a leg that brought it back to my mind was when Mr. Banks himself was putting his out of a taxi, when he got out of it after me, the day he took me to Sir Reginald's office."

Mr. Jellipot smiled with her at the absurdity of the idea. He said: "No, I don't think that would be sufficient to convict Mr. Banks. Identifications are often most unsatisfactory; and, unfortunately, everyone isn't as sensible, or as scrupulous as yourself.... I expect you'll be glad to see his office for the last time, and to forget that you've ever been in the enquiry business."

"Yes, I shall. But I should like to see it cleared up in such a way that my father's honour will be vindicated. I should like it proved what Mr. Rabone was."

"I think you may look on that as a very probable conclusion.... It seems that someone's been silly enough to kidnap young Hammerton, if they haven't done anything worse. I think that's where they've made a mistake."

Miss Weston waked to a more lively interest when she heard this. She asked for details, and Mr. Jellipot told what he knew, which was not much. "I wonder," he concluded, "whether I could ask you to do something more in this matter. Something that won't be dangerous if Peter Entwistle's innocent, as I am inclined to believe, but may be very dangerous if he isn't."

"Yes," she said, "if you say it's worth while, I'll do the best that I can."

"I ought to tell you first that the two matters may be quite separate. That the gang among whom Francis Hammerton got mixed up may have no connection with the Rabone murder. I think differently. I think they are more or less one. But I may be wrong."

"Very well. I understand that. I'll do anything you advise."

"I want you to find Peter Entwistle. I want you to tell him everything that led up to his arrest, from the angle of the Texall Enquiry Agency. If you think anything doesn't matter, or hesitate to mention it on other grounds, that's all the more reason why you should.

"When you've done that, say I want to see him, and bring him to me at once. It doesn't matter at what hour it may be. You'll have my private address on this card. You can memorize it, and tear it up."

"You won't tell me particularly what I'm to mention?"

"No. You'd better tell him naturally, in your own way. I may be quite wrong. And if I'm right, you'll be more likely to convince him if you haven't got the same idea in your mind."

"Am I to go now?"

"The sooner the better."

"You'll let Mr. Banks know that I shan't be back?"

"Did you leave a message that you were coming here?"

"No, I didn't. There was no one in that I cared to tell. The rule in that office is that we say the least that we can."

"It is an excellent one, which might with advantage be more widely applied. You can leave that to me."

Miss Weston went at that, without further words. She had a hurried meal in a nearby teashop, during which she considered how best she should approach Peter Entwistle, and what Mr. Jellipot could be particular that she should say. Then she got up briskly, paid her bill, and went out to call the first taxi she saw.

"Thirteen Vincent Street," she said, "and I want you to put me down without stopping to talk there, drive away for a few minutes, and then come back and stop a few doors farther down toward Windsor Terrace, on the other side, and wait for me there."

The man heard these instructions without enthusiasm, but his expression altered as she handed him a pound note.

"You can give me the change," she said, "if it comes to less, but it's quite likely there'll be something to add."

He listened with an intelligent interest as she went over the instructions again.

CHAPTER THIRTY-EIGHT

Mary Weston alighted at No. 13 Vincent Street, and walked up to a door that stood slightly open. Knowing something of its rather promiscuous hospitalities, she pushed it farther without the formality of using the bell, and ascended the stairs.

She must have used a more active and less obviously feminine tread than when she had crept down in the night, for as she reached the top landing, she heard Peter Entwistle's voice through a half-opened door: "If that's the taxi-man, call him in, and ask if he'll mind giving a hand. I could do with some help with this trunk."

The next moment Mrs. Musgrave appeared at the door. She had a hat on and a fur-collared coat, of a less sombre appearance than the clothes in which she had entered the witness-box little more than twenty-four hours earlier, and her expression was in even greater contrast, being one of excited animation, which changed to a puzzled doubt as she saw who her husband's visitor was.

"I can't say I'm a taxi-man," Miss Weston announced cheerfully, "but I don't mind lending a hand with a trunk, if you're needing a little help of that kind.

"I wanted a few words with Mr. Musgrave" (she remembered, just in time, that Peter's wife knew him by that name), "but it doesn't look as though I've chosen a good time to call."

She was through the door by this time, Mrs. Musgrave giving way somewhat doubtfully before her resolute, smiling advance.

The room showed sufficient evidence that Peter was on the

point of vacating it, and he made no secret of this when he looked up from his occupation of cording a heavy trunk, and saw who was there.

He had known nothing of Mary Weston two days before, but a man does not sit in the dock and hear a woman give evidence for two hours on which his liberty and perhaps his life may depend, without remembering face and voice.

"Glad to see you, Miss Weston," he said, "whatever has brought you here. You're only just in time, if you want to see me. There's a taxi ordered in half an hour, and I reckon we shall all be a bit older before anything will bring me to these rooms again."

"I did want to talk to you rather particularly, but I can see it's an awkward time."

"Ten minutes do? I can spare that, and a few more if necessary. I don't forget that I shouldn't be here, if you'd told your tale the least bit different from how you did."

"I only told the truth. You needn't thank me for that."

"Well, that's more than everyone tries to do, and some who do make it a muddled job.... Jean, there's some tea left in the pot, isn't there? You might give Miss Weston a cup."

Mary accepted this offer of hospitality, recognizing the inexpediency of saying that she had had a meal half an hour before. It settled her there for conversation for a few minutes, at least, which she must use to the best advantage she could.

"I should think," she said, "that you're wise to be getting away. I expect you've heard that Francis Hammerton's disappeared."

Peter Entwistle looked at her in a questioning manner, as though puzzled as to what the implication of this statement might be. She was aware that it was clumsily said, but she was feeling for an opening which was not easy to find.

"I don't see," he replied, "why he should clear out. He oughtn't to have had much to fear. Except, of course, that he'd got a sentence to serve. I'd forgotten that.... I shouldn't think he's gone far."

"I don't think he's gone willingly. Mr. Jellipot thinks he's been kidnapped, if nothing worse."

She thought that Peter Entwistle's manner became more reserved, if not hostile, as she said that. It was embarrassed, as it might have been had her conversation overstepped the limits of decency, in a way which his own politeness withheld him from observing openly.

He said: "Mr. Jellipot? Oh, yes, I know. He spoke up for Hammerton yesterday. Well, I hope he's wrong.... But Banks didn't send you here to tell me that Hammerton's disappeared."

He looked at her with a new suspicion in his mind, which she did not guess, but which was fortunately dissolved by her reply.

"No. It's nothing to do with Mr. Banks. It was Mr. Jellipot who asked me to see you."

(Was it right, she wondered, to mention that? But how could she tell what was right or wrong, being in the dark as she was. She could only go on talking, watching for a chance to say what she had been told.)

"Well, what does he want to know?"

"I'm not clear about that. In fact, he didn't say. I think he'd like to see you himself.... I suppose you've no idea who really did kill Mr. Rabone?"

Peter Entwistle looked at her without answering, but with an expression in which anger was not disguised, though bewilderment was more clearly indicated.

She thought: "He must have done it himself, and he supposes that I know." She remembered that Mr. Jellipot had said that if he were innocent she would be in no danger at all, but if he were guilty— Well, it was too late to draw back. She went on blunderingly.

"I think Mr. Jellipot's always been sure that it wasn't you, and Inspector Combridge never felt sure it was. It was Mr. Banks who would have it that it could be no one else, and of course, when you went away, it seemed to show he was right."

Peter Entwistle's face had become expressionless, as he asked: "I suppose he sees that he made a mistake now?"

She was conscious that the position had become menacing in some intangible way, and what might be wise or foolish to say was beyond her wits to decide. She must speak the truth as far as she could, and let the results be what they might. Being in the dark as she was, it was the simplest, and might be the wisest way.

"I don't know that he does," she answered. "I don't think Mr. Banks changes his opinion very easily. But Mr. Jellipot has never thought it was you, or, at least, that was the impression I got. Of course, if you could suggest who it was, it would make it clearer for you and Mr. Hammerton. It may be that Mr. Jellipot wanted to talk it over with you. But that's only a guess. I don't know."

"I've no time to see Mr. Jellipot. I'm going away. Did Mr. Banks tell you why he thought it was me?"

"I don't know that he had any reason except what was said in court. I mean about it being your window, and it being a left-handed man, and you going away. Oh, and you turning up when Mr. Hammerton was in court.

"I think that Mr. Banks attached special importance to that, because he'd said that, if you'd done it, you'd be sure to go to see Mr. Hammerton brought up. I don't understand why, but he felt sure, and I suppose the fact that he'd said you would, and then you did, influenced Inspector Combridge's mind."

Well, she had got it in, as she had promised she would. She had explained the matter from the angle of the Texall Enquiry Agency, and it looked as though all the satisfaction she would get would be that which comes from the sense of a promise kept, for Mr. Entwistle listened in a silence that became grimmer as she went on.

"It rather looks," he said, after a pause that left her vaguely afraid of she knew not what, "as though Mr. Banks were no friend to me?"

"No," she said, "but I don't suppose he felt any ill-will either. He just wanted to find out who murdered Mr. Rabone, and at that time he thought it was you."

He made no answer to that. He turned to his wife to say: "Jean, we're not going tonight. I've got to see Mr. Jellipot. You'd better go back to number eleven. I can phone you there."

Mrs. Musgrave looked troubled and bewildered, but she did not appear to be a wife who argued or required explanations under whatever circumstances. She said: "Yes, Peter. But don't be long."

He went without replying, and Mary followed him down the stairs.

When they reached the street, she saw her taxi waiting where she had arranged.

"I've got a taxi across the street," she said, when he would have turned the opposite way.

He looked at it, hesitated, and said: "No, thank you. I'll choose it myself, if you don't mind."

He led the way up the street while she reflected that the pound note might really prove to be an inadequate remuneration for the waiting driver.

She stopped, as a more sinister thought came to her mind. "I don't see," she said, "why I should trust you if you don't trust me."

He looked at her with the eyes of a man whose thoughts are on other things. Then he laughed. "No," he said, "I don't see why you should. We'd better both get on to a bus."

So they proceeded by that conveyance, and with a mutual feeling of recovered confidence, to Mr. Jellipot's house.

CHAPTER THIRTY-NINE

"What tickets?" Mr. Entwistle asked, as the conductor approached them, after they had climbed to the top of a Wimbledon bus.

"I'm not quite sure. All the way, I should think."

Mr. Entwistle didn't look pleased.

"Lawyer's office at Wimbledon?" he asked sceptically.

"No. Don't you see that it's nearer seven than six? Do you think we should find him at his office now?"

Mr. Entwistle took the tickets from a man whose impatience was becoming assertive, but he continued the subject.

"Know where he lives?"

"Yes, it's in Stagpole Road."

"Been there before?"

"No. But he gave me the address if we should be late."

Mr. Entwistle said no more. He appeared to find sufficient occupation in his own thoughts.

When they got down at Wimbledon he said: "Half a minute. I've got something to do."

He went into a telephone booth, and found Mr. Jellipot's name at the address which Miss Weston mentioned. Had he failed to do so, he had resolved to turn back.

He enquired from a policeman, and learned that Stagpole Road was nearly a mile away, on which he called a taxi, which, seeing assurance of her own safety in the mood of suspicion which he displayed, Mary made no objection to entering. So they came safely at last to Mr. Jellipot's door.

The mode of travelling which Mr. Entwistle had preferred had not been the fastest possible, and Mr. Jellipot had finished dinner and was enjoying the evening cigar which was the one vice of his bachelor solitude, when his visitors were announced.

He received them with his usual quiet cordiality, and the timid, somewhat hesitant, manner which concealed the unhurried working of a very capable brain.

"I am particularly pleased to see you, Mr. Entwistle," he said, "because your coming assures me that you had no part in William Rabone's murder, which was an opinion I had already formed, and ventured, with some diffidence, to express to those who are most conversant with such problems, and consequently more capable of their solution than I can ever expect to be. And it also leads me to hope that another theory that I have formed, but on which I scarcely ventured to build, it being as conjectural as it was, may not be entirely unfounded.... You will take a glass of wine, Miss Weston? And you, Mr. Entwistle? No? You may be right, for your work calls for a steady hand."

The length of this somewhat involved, and yet fundamentally lucid statement, had given time for Peter Entwistle to settle comfortably in the softly upholstered chair which Mr. Jellipot had indicated for his use, and relieved him of the necessity of immediate speech. It gave him the satisfaction of knowing that he would be speaking to a lawyer whose mind had no lingering doubt of whether he were himself a party to the crime for which he was about to denounce another; and the final words, the implication of which he was quick to guess, confirmed an opinion already formed that Mr. Jellipot was of a more astute and more militant quality, than his manner showed.

Mr. Jellipot, still in no haste to approach the subject in all their minds, asked by what means they had come, and being told that they had utilized the services of a Wimbledon bus, he had a moment of gravity.

"It was," he said, "a rather bold thing to do."

Peter Entwistle, who had considered it in a contrary light, looked uncomprehendingly at this criticism, and Mr. Jellipot expounded it further.

"I suppose," he said, "you felt a doubt as to whether Miss Weston might be a decoy to lead you into a position of further compromise, or even more acute and imminent danger. I do not blame you for that. Whether or not you believed what she must have told you, it remained a possibility which you would wish to eliminate from a position already sufficiently hazardous. But did you think how easily, by the method you chose, you could be followed here by those whom you will have, in fact, a greater reason to dread?"

"No," Peter admitted, "I can't say that I thought of that."

Mr. Jellipot shook his head slightly over the ill-judging reck-lessness of the young, and recovered cheerfulness to observe that, as no one could have foreseen that Miss Weston would be calling upon him, or the purpose with which she went, the damage might not have been very great.

His next words went to the heart of the subject which had brought Peter Entwistle there, and saved him the task of prelim-inary explanation. "I needn't ask you to tell me," he said, "who killed William Rabone. Your coming here is sufficient answer to that. What I should like to know is whether you have, or could obtain, anything in the nature of legal proof, or whether it will be necessary to make the arrest on the minor charge.

"I need not tell you that you yourself will now be in great jeopardy till the arrest is made; nor that Inspector Combridge will be particularly cautious to avoid making a third arrest till he is very sure of his ground.... I should add that I have asked him to be with us at ten o'clock, or as soon after as possible, so that you should be brief in anything that you may wish to say before he arrives, or if—against which, for your own sake, I should wish to dissuade you very strongly—you should prefer to leave without seeing him."

Mr. Entwistle, thinking that the precept of brevity was some-what contrary to the example which Mr. Jellipot set, was at last given an opportunity of reply. "I don't know," he said, "what you'll call legal proof, but I can give you enough evidence to put him away for ten years on the London & Northern frauds, and I should think you'd do best to begin on that. You'll find it's easier to get evidence on the Rabone case after he's arrested, unless I'm wrong.... But as to going before the inspector comes, there's no man that I'm more anxious to see.... Does he expect that he'll find me here?"

"No. It was a suggestion that I felt I had no right to make until I had more to go on than what might have seemed to other minds an improbable guess. He will be coming here to let me know what he's been able to do to trace Francis Hammerton. I did venture to tell him that I might have something helpful to contribute from my side."

"I don't know that I can help you in that. It depends upon what the Inspector knows."

"He knew nothing this morning, but he won't have been idle since then." And having said that, Mr. Jellipot turned the conversation to other topics. He was complimentary to Mr. Entwistle's wife. He expressed satisfaction when he learned that she had a life-interest in some property in Scotland, to which they meant to retire. He approved Mr. Entwistle's explanation that he had cultivated too many branches of manual art in the past, and had decided that excellence would be more probably attained if he should confine himself to landscape painting, which, in future, he was determined to do. It was still a few minutes to ten when Inspector Combridge was shown into the room.

CHAPTER FORTY

"I think," Mr. Jellipot said, "that you may speak without reserve before Mr. Entwistle, who may be able to supplement any knowledge you have obtained."

The Inspector looked the surprise he felt, but he had a well-founded confidence in Mr. Jellipot's discretion. He said: "We've found out a bit, thanks to a good man who happened to be on his beat in Deal Street last night.

"He'd happened to see Hammerton in court when he was sentenced, and he recognized him going into a restaurant which hasn't a very good reputation, at about seven last night.

"I had an interesting hour with the proprietor, and then with two of the waiters, and in the end I got this. Francis Hammerton dined there with Augusta Garten and two other men. One of the men left early. They can't or won't say who he was, and they've given me one of those general descriptions that mean nothing at all. It's no use searching London for a tall dark man in a grey suit, and with a habit of wearing spats.

"The other man was an ex-officer named Driver, about whom we know a good deal and not much that's good. He was cashiered from one of the Guards regiments after he'd been caught cheating at cards.

"Hammerton and Miss Garten left with him in his car about 9:45 P.M. and they didn't go to the house in Hounslow where he has been lying low since we caught Tony Welch.

"Where they did go is what we've failed to find out as yet. But we know the number of Driver's car, and we're having a good look-out for it all over the south of England."

Mr. Jellipot turned to Entwistle to ask: "Can you give us any idea where Driver was most likely to go?"

Peter Entwistle did not answer that. He asked Inspector Combridge: "May I put a question to you first?"

"You may if you like. I can't promise to answer before I hear it."

"I want to know why you were waiting for me with a warrant for my arrest in Mr. Garrison's court. Did you expect me to be there when Hammerton was put in the dock?"

"Yes, I did. I thought at that time that you were the criminal, and there is a common belief that the actual murderer is unable to keep away when another man is being prosecuted for his crime."

"Yes. I've heard that gag. I don't know whether it's true. May I ask you just one thing more? Did you have that idea yourself, or did someone else put it into your mind?"

The Inspector hesitated. He disliked being questioned by Peter Entwistle, and if he replied further he wished to be sure that he would receive payment in kind.

"If I answer that, do I understand that you will tell me how Francis Hammerton can be found?"

"No. He may be dead. But I'll tell you the best way to save him if he's still alive. And if you give me the answer I expect, I'll tell you who murdered Rabone."

"It was Mr. Banks who made the suggestion to me."

"Did he say he thought I was guilty?"

"Yes. He held that opinion. So did I at the time."

"What does he say now?"

"I believe he has that opinion still."

"The low hound! He murdered Rabone himself."

Inspector Combridge's look of surprise approached incredulity. "It is a statement which would require evidence in its support."

"Miss Fortescue saw him leaving, just before Miss Weston came down the stairs. He gave her a hundred pounds not to squeal."

"Any evidence besides that?"

"No. I don't know that I have. But who else would it be likely to be?"

"I can't answer that. I don't know why it should be likely to be him. It sounds unlikely to me. If you knew this, why didn't you tell us before?"

"Because I'm not that kind of rat. He'd have been safe with me if you'd offered a thousand pounds "

"As a matter of fact, Sir Reginald Crowe's offering twice that amount."

"Then it's likely you'll get all the evidence you require. But you won't buy it from me. I didn't know it was he, though I might have guessed without overworking my brain. But I didn't guess that he'd planned to frame it on me, as I know he has now, and that's why I'm sitting here."

"How do you know that now?"

"It was he who advised me to clear out. He said the police were looking for me over an old matter that's—it doesn't matter about that now. I believed what he said. I'd no idea that I was under any suspicion in the Rabone case."

"You mean Mr. Banks told you himself to go in hiding from us?"

"I don't mean he said it face to face. He passed me the word."

"And then told you to come to the court when Hammerton was brought up?"

"I was to be there to meet one of the gang who was to give me the tip about the Leatherhead—it doesn't matter what it was about now."

Inspector Combridge was interested, but still less than convinced. He said: "If you could give me the least idea why Banks should have wanted to murder Rabone, or get you into the dock "

"Because he was the one who organized the bank frauds, and he knew that Rabone was going to give him away."

"That," Mr. Jellipot said modestly, "was what I had concluded to be the case."

Hearing the assurance in his voice, Inspector Combridge began to place a new value on this incredible tale. He asked Entwistle: "You can prove this, I suppose?"

"Oh, yes. I can prove that. I can give you the names of half a dozen who'll be all the evidence that you'll need when they know what he tried doing to me, so long as you promise not to make it too hot for them."

"It seems to me," Mr. Jellipot said quietly, "that you should arrest Banks before he gets any idea that suspicion has been directed upon him."

"It's the one chance for Augusta Garten and Mr. Hammerton," Entwistle said, "if it's not too late now, as it most probably is."

Inspector Combridge did not reply. He looked worried. A third arrest without justification would be a comedy which even his established reputation would not survive. And it was an absurdly improbable tale, based on no more than Peter Entwistle's word, which an impartial judgement might not value at a high price.

Well, to be fair, he had said that Miss Fortescue could give it some support. Another witness of the kind that is likely to do more harm than good to the side which dares to put them into the box!

And even if it could be shown that Banks was at No. 13 Vincent Street on the night in question, it was a long distance from establishing him as the author of the crime four doors away. Was he not commissioned by the London & Northern Bank to watch a number of suspicious characters of whom Peter Entwistle was one? He might have been there with good reason enough, and it was consistent with his reputation for reticence that he should not have mentioned the fact.

Mr. Jellipot, who understood his thoughts very well, broke the silence by observing: "It isn't Mr. Entwistle's evidence alone on which you have to depend. Miss Weston recognized Mr. Banks's leg as he left the scene of the crime. She only hesitated to say this because it seemed such an improbable thing."

The Inspector turned to Miss Weston, who had listened silently to this conversation, as a drowning man looks for a rope. "That a fact, Miss Weston?" he asked. "I thought it was the same when I saw Mr. Banks put his out of a taxi, but it seemed too absurd to mention. It was the spats I noticed particularly—"

"Oh, spats!" Inspector Combridge recalled that these articles had been present in that description the vagueness of which he had lamented a few minutes before.

He said: "I think I shall give myself the pleasure of asking Mr. Banks a few questions."

"I think," Mr. Jellipot suggested, "if you put the handcuffs on him first, he'd be more likely to answer quietly."

"Yes, I daresay he would. But wouldn't he make a noise when I found I'd got to take them off him again? It's easy for you to talk. You've no one to tell you when you go wrong."

Mr. Jellipot, observing that the irritation of indecision had taken the inspector to the verge of incivility, had the discretion to avoid a direct reply.

He said mildly: "As I reconstruct the event—an operation in which I admit that my inexperience may cause me to overlook points which would be evident at once to your more experienced mind—the case has the simplicity which I am accustomed to associate with correct deduction.

"It is one of the difficulties of all large-scale criminals that they must have some legitimate place in the world sufficient to explain their financial resources, and to provide them with an ostensible occupation, such as will prevent suspicion being inclined toward them.

"In Jesse Banks I see no reason to doubt that we have identified the man who controlled and financed both the frauds upon the London & Northern Bank, and the somewhat different activities of the gang which you have, for the moment, scattered and frightened by the arrest and conviction of Tony Welch.

"The occupation selected by Banks for the world to see was of a kind which might be expected from the abilities which such a man must possess. It enabled him to keep in friendly touch with your own department, to obtain much knowledge which he could use if suspicion approached his friends, and to have a legitimate excuse if he should be overseen among criminal associates.

"It enabled him, in particular, to obtain the appointment from the London & Northern Bank of investigation of the very frauds which he financed and directed, and, in particular, it must have enabled him, while following Sir Reginald's instructions to place Miss Weston where she could cultivate the acquaintance of William Rabone, to warn him of her intentions, so that it would be unlikely that he would give her any dangerous confidences.

"It is reasonable to suppose that he became doubtful of William Rabone's loyalty—the bank inspector may have become alarmed at the vigour of the investigations which Sir Reginald's energy had instituted—and that he visited him in that secret manner with the object of reassurance, or of finally disposing of a man whose confession would have been ruinous to himself.

"Rabone may—but this is no more than a guess—have mentioned that an escaped convict was in the house, and have so made his fate more certain, as it showed that there was another man on whom suspicion might naturally fall.

"I suppose that it was with that object that Banks robbed the man he had murdered, which he could otherwise have had no occasion to do, and so caused the moment's delay which enabled Miss Weston to arrive on the scene before he had disappeared.

"Had Mr. Hammerton acted in a less natural—or less innocent—way, he might now be awaiting trial for a crime in which he had no part whatever."

Inspector Combridge listened to this theory of the crime with the close and critical attention of one who was expert in the details of such deductions, and who desired nothing so much as that the truth should be found, by whatever means.

He had no professional jealousy of Mr. Jellipot, with whom

he had been previously associated in investigation of the criminal practices of Professor Blinkwell, in which they had learned a mutual respect and friendship, but he had the caution of one who has blundered twice already in a business in which such blunders cannot be lightly condoned.

"It sounds plausible," he said, "when you put it like that; but what about the crime having been the work of a left-handed man?"

"I suggest that Banks deliberately used his left hand, so that suspicion might fall upon Mr. Entwistle, rather than himself."

"And you think he would risk Entwistle giving him away when he found himself threatened with the capital charge for a murder with which he had had nothing to do?"

"Yes. I think he did. And I think the course of events showed that he could have done it with safety, so long as Mr. Entwistle had no cause to think that he was instigating or assisting the prosecution; or probably anything more than a vague guess—if that—as to who the actual criminal was."

"But I don't think he anticipated that Mr. Entwistle would be prosecuted, or perhaps even suspected. He would have preferred that it should remain an unsolved mystery, or been attributed to Hammerton's desperate need for funds—robbery leading to murder, as it so frequently does. It was only as an additional insurance against detection that he struck with the razor in his left hand.

"To use an apposite metaphor, he did not wish the lightning to come in his direction, but he provided a lightning-conductor, in the person of Mr. Entwistle, as a precaution against it if it should.

"He must have gone quietly up the stairs of No. 13, a house where many feet would pass with little notice during the night, and knowing that he could make a good excuse if he were observed to enter.

"Had he not been noticed by one of the women on the lower floor as he left, and had not Miss Weston followed him to the window by which he retreated, he would not have thought that it would be conducive to his own security to encourage the idea of Mr. Entwistle's guilt.... And, of course, even then he would not have done so, had he known of the alibi by which the accusation could be rebuffed.

"Had Mr. Entwistle been in his room that night, I doubt whether he would have improved his position by accusing Banks, even had he been prepared to defend himself on those lines. He would have had to denounce Banks in his capacity as the alleged head of a criminal gang, and to explain his knowledge of, and association with him, so that the motive of the murder might be established, and in the end he would most probably have been wrongly convicted himself as a party to, if not as the actual perpetrator, of the crime. He might have succeeded in involving Banks, had his accusations been credited, but he would have done no good for himself.

"I think any solicitors—and certainly those he had instructed—would have advised him that he had a better chance of acquittal if he should deny everything, and throw the onus of legal proof entirely upon the prosecution.

"He was saved by the fact that he was not in his room that night; and Banks has only come to his present jeopardy because I have been able to convey to Mr. Entwistle the fact that he has been what is, I believe, colloquially known as double-crossed by one whom he should have been able to trust."

The Inspector considered this, and saw two flaws in a reconstruction with which he was otherwise inclined to agree.

"There's Bigland's evidence," he said. "You must get over that."

"I don't think that's a point about which we should worry much. I never did take it very seriously, beyond that it showed that Miss Weston really had gone down the stairs in the night, which there had never been any reason to doubt.

"Did you ever know an authentic case of a man lying awake all night? No doubt there are such, but the number of people who think they have done so must be a hundred times as numerous. He may have told the truth as far as he knew. Actually, if he were restless, and inclined to wake easily, he would be more likely to notice a woman's step, which was unusual upon those stairs, than that of a man, which was an accustomed sound."

"Yes, I should say that's likely enough," the Inspector answered, "but what do you make of Banks risking the murder with Miss Weston in the next room? He knew she was in the house. He almost certainly knew where she slept. He had received her report that she had followed someone—probably himself—over the slates before."

"I agree about that," Mr. Jellipot conceded readily, "but there are one or two points which may be taken into consideration, and which diminish its force.

"In the first place, I suppose that his position was desperate. If Rabone told him, as he probably did, that it was too late to argue; perhaps even that he had already written to his general manager, and so giving him no more than a few hours to clear out, he must have known that it was then or never, and anger against the man who had resolved to betray him may have strengthened the impulse of self-preservation which urged the crime.

"But it is probable that he may not have regarded Miss Weston as so great a danger to his security as she proved to be.

"He may have planned to kill his victim by a blow so sudden that no cry would have left his lips. The ferocity of the two cuts supports this conclusion, and it is probable that his purpose was only defeated by his own subtlety. The first stroke almost reached to where the larynx would have been severed beyond the possibility of an articulate cry, and had it been struck with the full force of his right—that is, with his accustomed—hand it is probable that William Rabone would have fallen without a sound which could have been heard by a woman presumably asleep in the next room.

"And if, as was normally probable, she had been asleep, and almost certainly undressed at that hour, he might have thought that there would be little danger that she could have followed him promptly enough even to detect the window to which he fled. And against that remote risk he provided, as far as circumstances allowed, when he struck a left-handed blow."

CHAPTER FORTY-ONE

Inspector Combridge looked half-convinced. He said: "It looks as though there won't be much bed for me. I think I'll go back to the Yard, and see whether it's not too late to have a consultation on this before morning. I'm not going to make another arrest off my own bat.... Tomorrow, it's likely I may give Mr. Banks a call."

Mr. Jellipot looked his dissatisfaction. "There's such a thing as being cautious at the wrong time."

"So there is. And there are risks that are worse than that. What real evidence have we got? I daresay I shall interview Gracie Fortescue during the night. Fortunately, she's a lady who keeps late hours."

Inspector Combridge got up to go.

But Mr. Jellipot held to his point, with his usual mild-mannered tenacity. "And if you lose your principal witness by the delay? You can't suppose Mr. Entwistle's life will be very safe if they learn that he's been two hours talking with us?"

"There'll be no risk about that. Peter's coming with me."

Mr. Entwistle, who had a lively sense of the peril in which he stood, proved to be a willing party to this arrangement. He offered to spend the night in the compilation of a written state-ment of a more voluntary character than those curious docu-ments usually are.

He only required the previous use of Mr. Jellipot's telephone, to inform his wife that they would not be leaving for Scotland as promptly as they had planned, but that there would be no need for alarm if he were not home during the night.

While he was at the instrument, Mr. Jellipot did not fail to remember that his own client was Francis Hammerton, and that his interests had not yet received the attention which he considered that they required.

He asked: "What are you going to do about Hammerton and the German woman?"

"I don't know what more I can do tonight. You may be sure the search won't be relaxed. I hope, when we've got Entwistle's statement, there'll be some pointers in that."

"I should have thought that you would have asked him that first."

Inspector Combridge, whose mind was sufficiently occupied at the moment with other aspects of the problem which confronted him, took Mr. Jellipot's unusual acerbity with a good-humoured smile."

"So I will," he said. "If he can tell me where Driver would be most likely to go to earth, it might be useful in more ways than one."

As he spoke, Peter Entwistle came back from the adjoining room, in which the telephone was situated. He said: "They cut me off rather short. There's a call for you, Inspector."

Inspector Combridge went to the instrument, and after a short but lively conversation, in which his voice could be heard giving instructions with an animation suggestive of active and favourable developments, he came back to say: "We haven't got to run after Driver. Beddoes caught him in a Greek Street restaurant where he had been sitting for two hours, apparently waiting, for someone who didn't come. Beddoes wouldn't take him till he got up to go, hoping that some more fish might walk into the net. It's some comfort to think that we've got one good man in the force. I'm not sure that I oughtn't to recommend him to take my place when I resign in about two days' time, as I'm most likely to do.... We've got no charge against Driver, except that he was in possession of firearms without a licence, but they can hold him for questioning for a few hours, and I daresay

Peter'll give us the right dope before we have to bring him up in the morning.... And that brings me to what I promised to ask. Can you give me a pointer to where, if he's still alive, they'd be most likely to have Hammerton hidden away?"

"No, I can't say that I know. But if Colonel Driver's under arrest, you'll do well to have Cuckford watched. But I suppose you know all about that."

Inspector Combridge was obliged to say that the name conveyed no useful idea to his mind. Peter Entwistle, who was accustomed to credit the police with more omniscience than they possess, as most criminals are inclined to do, was more surprised than he would have considered it good manners to show.

"It's the Flying School at Cuckford, I mean," he explained. "I don't know who's supposed to own it, but it's under Driver's control. If you get Banks, or any of the others, badly alarmed, and don't run them in, you'll find that they won't risk Croydon. They'll put off from Cuckford without the formality of having their passports examined."

"That's a good tip," the Inspector answered, and, perhaps not illogically, the statement gave him more confidence than he had felt previously that he was not on the wrong track for a third time. "Thanks, Jellipot," he added generously, recognizing that it was the lawyer's urgency which had brought that information so promptly before him.

He went at that, with Peter Entwistle in his company. On arriving at the Yard he made him comfortable there, with refreshments appropriate to the occasion, and the writing materials that were equally indicated.

He had a hurried consultation with such of his colleagues as were available at that hour, with results somewhat discouraging to himself, and then gave certain instructions which resulted in the local police-sergeant at Cuckford remaining on duty long after his usual hours, and two cars of plainclothes men, to whom firearms had been served out, leaving half an hour later, on the Cuckford road.

After that, he went out to interview Miss Gracie Fortescue, whom he was fortunate enough to find without much difficulty, and when she understood that he came in peace, and was not proposing to subject her to one of those periodic arrests by which she was required to share her earnings with the authorities of the State, she made little difficulty, finding how much he already knew, of a frank disclosure of the circumstances under which she had received a substantial bribe from Mr. Jesse Banks.

She said that he had been more expeditious than the Inspector (having a more direct and evident reason) in interviewing her after the murder. He had told her that he had been engaged in a secret investigation of great importance on behalf of the London & Northern Bank, and that it was essential that, if she were questioned by anyone, she should not disclose that he had been there during the night.

He had accompanied this statement with the enormous-seeming bribe of a hundred pounds, which he had implied was from funds placed in his hands by the bank (from which source Inspector Combridge saw that it might actually have been drawn), and that the importance of the matter at issue made this a relatively trifling amount.

At that time, she had not supposed that his presence at No. 13 could have any connection with a murder four doors away, and had accepted the money without anticipation that she might be drawing trouble upon herself, especially as she understood that Mr. Banks was of the nature of a police officer himself, and in the confidence or the force.

When the inspector had questioned her subsequently, she had not mentioned an incident which she had already pledged herself to conceal, and which she honestly thought to have no connection with the matter to which his own enquiries were directed.

Such was her tale, and when she found that she was neither to be involved in trouble for what she had failed to disclose on the earlier occasion, nor required to disgorge the money, she readily undertook to make a written statement in confirmation of the account she had given.

CHAPTER FORTY-TWO

The Cuckford Aviation and Instructional Company Limited owned a track of moorland country several hundred acres in extent, which lay, level and high, about three miles from the ancient village from which its name was derived.

It took flying pupils, for whom it provided a service of cars to bring and return them from their Cuckford lodgings, as there was no nearer accommodation. The company's buildings consisted of a canteen, some hangars of considerable extent, and a range of barrack-like edifices which provided lodging for the permanent staff.

In separate rooms in these buildings, too closely watched for opportunity of escape, Augusta Garten and Francis had been confined, without opportunity for communications to pass between them.

They had been brought there at a late hour of the previous night, each in a closed car, and with an armed guard sitting on either hand, after they had been subjected to some preliminary questioning at the Berkshire residence of a man whom Francis heard addressed as Captain Morgan, and who was known to Miss Garten by some other names in addition, without certainty as to which, if any, had been his original property.

After arrival at Cuckford, Miss Garten had been further questioned by this gentleman and some other of her previous associates. The examination had not been unfriendly, and appeared to be genuinely concerned to arrive at the truth of her relations with Francis, and of her continued loyalty to the gang, and she had sustained it with sufficient success to feel some expectation that she would recover their shaken confidence, until, as the evening advanced, Captain Morgan entered her room with an expression such as she had not seen on his face before, and asked curtly: "What was the meaning of 'Don't come' in the letter you sent to Hammerton two days ago?"

The question was so abrupt, and its substance so unexpected, that even her practised duplicity could not conceal the first moment of consternation, but she recovered herself instantly to reply: "I don't know what you mean. I never sent any letter at all."

"And that is the only explanation you have?"

"It seems to me to be a complete answer."

Captain Morgan turned, with no further word, and went out of the room. He left her wondering how that letter could have come to his knowledge, unless Francis himself had revealed it, in a last desperate effort to save himself from the danger in which he lay, and even that explanation failed when she recalled that he had only heard of it from her, and could have no exact knowledge of the wording which Captain Morgan had quoted so accurately. But if they knew for a fact that she had sent such a communication, she saw that the last hope of mercy was surely gone.

Francis, meanwhile, had been subjected to a different ordeal. He had been offered release, or, at least, to be handed over to the care of the local Cuckford police, if he would make a written confession of his complicity in the crime for which he had been convicted, and the penalty of refusal had been plainly stated.

"If you are so unreasonable as to refuse," Captain Morgan had said, "you will put me to the unpleasant necessity of assisting you to escape from the penalty of the law. We must provide you with a machine in which you can attempt to cross the Channel to such safety as may be found on the other side. We can start you off, but you will see that we cannot afterwards navigate the machine. If you should fall into the sea, which I fear would be a very probable end of your adventure, you will see that you will have perished in the endeavour to flee from an appeal in the merits of which men will suppose that you had no belief, and they will judge it to be the act of a guilty man.

"Why not therefore save your life by a confession which will place you in no worse position?"

Stated so, it was a hard thing to refuse, and he might not have rejected the temptation to write and then endeavour to repudiate such a document, had he not felt a natural distrust of the good faith in which the proposal was made. Might it not be that they desired to obtain it from him for their own security, before they sent him to dreadful death?

It was at a late hour of the winter night when he was roused from such sleep as his condition allowed, to be told to dress, as he would now be permitted to leave at once.

He was led, with a pistol-muzzle against his back, to one of the smaller hangars, which were for the renting of those who kept their own private planes at the aerodrome.

He looked up at a machine which was, in fact, of the larger size, and which seemed immense to his unaccustomed eyes, which had only seen such monsters before as they passed far over his head, or in pictures upon the screen.

He looked round in the vain hope of escape, or for someone to whom he might make what his reason told him would be no more than useless appeal, and saw Augusta Garten, similarly guarded, a few paces away.

She returned his glance, and saw in his eyes the desperation of fear. Better, he thought, to die in a useless struggle there, to make one last effort of breaking free, to be shot down if he must, rather than to be sent aloft to that certain and dreadful death. She said: "It's no use, Harold. We've got to go. There's no other way," and he found himself calmed and steadied by the dull hopelessness of her voice, and by a sense of companionship in misery that it gave. He felt as though he would be deserting her at her equal need, if he should endeavour to break away.

All this was in an instant of time, for their captors were in a great haste. They saw, to their surprise, a pilot climb into the machine. They were pushed and hurried into seats at his rear.

They could not guess that the occasion for haste was that Inspector Beddoes was known to have already stopped at the Cuckford police station, and now to be on the point of starting his cars on the three miles of road still separating him from the aerodrome, which four minutes would be sufficient to cover. They heard the whirr of the propeller. Slowly, heavily, but at ever-increasing speed, the machine moved out on to the field, and rose into the darkness.

Inspector Beddoes saw it go, and supposed ruefully that he had missed his intended prey. He did not see the pilot drop by parachute from the machine when he had taken it to a sufficient height, and headed it on a southern course. He left it rising slightly but steadily into the wind, with sufficient petrol in its tank to take it well out over the sea.

CHAPTER FORTY-THREE

Inspector Beddoes was a sanguine and resolute officer. He did not consider the possibility of failure so much as the results of success, if he should become a prominent instrument in rooting out a gang on whose tracks he had been for the past two years, with no more result as yet than that Tony Welch was behind prison bars for a number of years to come.

If we contrast his conduct with the hesitations of Inspector Combridge, we must in justice observe that he had no more than a subordinate responsibility, that he had not the burden of two mistaken arrests on his record in this case already, and that he had more to gain and less to lose than his superior officer, whose brilliant record could more easily be sullied by conspicuous failure than brightened by one additional triumph.

Finding the aerodrome to be in a condition of activity unusual for the night hours, he had no scruple in surrounding it, and placing everyone he found on the premises under detention while he commenced his investigations.

He was told at once that Captain Morgan was in control, and he proceeded to question him.

"I understand that you are in charge here?"

"In Colonel Driver's absence, yes."

"You have had a young man here named Francis Hammerton?"

This was a random shot, which was lucky to find its mark, and Inspector Beddoes had additional cause for surprise when he received a frank and affirmative answer.

"Yes, if that be his real name. He came here under that of

Vaughan, with a young woman named Garten, with whom he appeared to be on rather intimate terms. He wanted to hire a plane, which I was unwilling to let him have. I should say that Miss Garten is, more or less, an acquaintance of Colonel Driver. She's been here before, and no doubt it was she who brought him.

"I learned that he was a convict with a bad record, and though he said he was out on bail, I had no confirmation even of that.

"I made excuse that we must have a large deposit before letting him have a machine out, and though he offered to pay it, it was by cheque, which I said we must have time to clear.

"I suppose they knew you were on their track. Anyway, they've stolen a plane, and bolted only a few minutes ago. I expect you saw them as you came, heading out to the sea."

Inspector Beddoes listened to this explanation with a face which gave no sign of his thoughts. He said only: "I expect I shall have further instructions by morning. In the meantime, I am taking charge here. You can all get back to bed."

CHAPTER FORTY-FOUR

Inspector Combridge was in the office of the Assistant-Commissioner.

Sir William Ingleby had discussed the Rabone murder with him for the last hour, and his decision was still to come.

"It isn't that I don't trust you, Combridge," he said. "I don't suppose we've got a sounder officer in the force, or one on whose judgement I should be more pleased to rely. But I can see that you're not certain yourself, and after what has happened already—well, the press and the public have been kinder than we've deserved, but everyone's watching now to see that we bring the thing to a satisfactory end, and a third mistake might be more than some of us could survive.

"As to the tale of how Hammerton got away, I'm with you when you say it leaves a lot to explain, but, after all, it's quite a possible thing. You must remember that he asked you to leave him unwatched on the night when he started his flight. At the most, I don't see how you can go further today than inviting Banks to call in and clear up one or two matters like that hundred pounds bribe, which I daresay he'll be quite equal to doing. Of course, when you've had time to verify some of Entwistle's allegations, you may be on stronger grounds. But even there we've got to remember that they are made by a man who admits his own criminal practices, by implication at least, and who is not free from suspicion of being the murderer."

"Yes, I admit all that, sir," Inspector Combridge answered stubbornly. He had made up his own mind, perhaps the more firmly for the time which that process had required, and was resolved that the hesitation of his Chief must not frustrate the full success of the coup on which he had now determined.

He said: "From the telephone conversation I've had with Sir Reginald, I reckon it won't be many hours before he'll have checked up on Entwistle's statements sufficiently to give us all the proof we shall need at this stage. We needn't put the Rabone case to the front till we can see further ahead, but I've got a feeling that—"

It was a sentence he was not destined to finish, for he was interrupted by an announcement that Mr. Jesse Banks had called, and would like to see him.

"I'd better go, sir?" he asked.

"No. I think not. We'll have him here. It's not fair to leave all the responsibility on your shoulders. I'll talk to him myself, and then tell you what I've decided to do."

Inspector Combridge could make no objection to this, though he saw that Sir William's decision was capable of an interpretation less flattering to himself than that which had been expressed.

The next moment, Mr. Banks, looking his usual calm and taciturn self, entered the room.

Certainly, Sir William thought, he had no aspect of criminality. His manner was that of a man whose mind was at ease, and there was somewhat more than usual of friendliness in his tone as he said: "I hear you've got Driver. You can always reckon on Beddoes to make his catch if he once gets on the trail. I meant to be first for once, but I suppose it's you that will be in at the death... It's your organization that's bound to beat any private office."

Sir William Ingleby interposed before Inspector Combridge could reply.

"Mr. Banks," he said, "you are a gentleman of good reputation, and when aspersions against any such come from criminal mouths, we are very slow to believe. But we often think it well to inform those who are traduced in such ways, so that the facts may be properly ascertained, and no lingering suspicion may remain against them.

"It is due to you to say that during the last twenty-four hours you have been the subject of allegations of the most serious kind, which your very opportune call will doubtless help us to dispose of as they deserve."

He went on to narrate the nature and extent of these accusations, not shrinking from a sufficient bluntness, and yet putting them in an impersonal and putative manner, at which it would not be easy for an innocent man to take offence.

Mr. Banks listened without interruption, and with no more sign of feeling than a slight smile which crossed his face at times as the more monstrous of these charges appeared.

"I suppose," he said easily, when the recital was concluded, "that you wish me to make a formal denial of these allegations, as, of course, I do. But," and his manner changed to that of a faint contempt as he turned to the inspector, "I always knew you were jealous of what I do, but I didn't think you'd fall into such a mug's trap as that.

"Of course, I've been mixing myself up with the Driver gang. How do you suppose a private detective gets along? Of course, I didn't want you to know I'd been at No. 13 that night. I like to go my own way, without interference from you, and in this case I thought it cheap at the price

"I daresay Sir Reginald would have done too, if you'd left me to complete what I was doing. But, anyway, it's between him and me, and if he disallows the payment, I daresay I can stand the loss.

"I think that's the only point that deserves an answer in the whole tale. I've helped you to bring Entwistle to justice, which he's been too clever to let you do in the last ten years, and when he turns on me, you're foolish enough to swallow the hook."

There was a moment's silence as he concluded. Sir William, more than half convinced that they had heard the contemptuous protest of an innocent man, and recognizing that his defence was largely a repetition of the arguments he had himself been urging upon the inspector before Mr. Banks entered the room, looked at his subordinate officer to see what effect it had had on his mind.

Inspector Combridge saw that if he stood his ground, and was wrong, he would be discredited beyond further remedy. He may be excused if there was a moment of hesitation during which his reply paused, and in that instant Sir William's telephone rang.

"Mr. Jellipot?" they heard him say. "Oh yes, the Rabone matter, of course. And *who did you say*? Well, show them up." He laid the receiver down as he said: "Mr. Jellipot, Mr. Hammerton's lawyer, is here. I thought we had better see him together."

As he spoke, Mr. Jellipot entered the room, with Francis Hammerton and Augusta Garten behind him.

Mr. Jellipot paused when he saw the visitor that Sir William already had. He took no notice of the amazed expressions of those who observed the two who followed him into the room. He said, in his precise and almost diffident manner: "It is most opportune that Mr. Banks should be with us now. It will save trouble all round. It is my painful duty to charge him with the attempted murder of—"

He was interrupted by the voice of the man of whom he spoke, which had changed its tone to one of peremptory order.

"I've heard enough of this. Hands up, if you think your lives are worth keeping." He added sharply: "I shan't warn you again." His eyes as he spoke were on Inspector Combridge and the Assistant Commissioner, whom he doubtless recognized as his most formidable opponents, and the last words were for the Inspector, who had shown a dangerous reluctance to accept the ignominy that obedience must entail both upon himself and the force to which he belonged.

It is difficult to give equal attention to several people at once who are not all at the same side of the room, and it may be in that that Mr. Jellipot saw his opportunity, but his own explanation was that he acted from an impulse of fear alone.

He had not yet been asked to take a seat, and he was standing beside a table on which there was a carafe of water, very similar to that which had been overset on the occasion of Francis Hammerton's escape from custody a few weeks before.

There seems to be some faint suggestion of poetic justice, very difficult to analyse, in the second appearance of one of these articles at the present crisis.

However that be, the fact was that Mr. Jellipot caught the bottle by the neck, and hurled it with considerable force at Mr. Banks's face, against which it broke, with results which were not conducive to rapid and accurate shooting by a man whose previous practice was of a very occasional kind.

He did fire twice, but the shots did no damage, except to the substantial furniture into which they sank, and before there was time for a further discharge, Inspector Combridge had tripped up a man who was stumbling half-blindly toward the door.

Sir William Ingleby looked coolly round a somewhat disordered room, as the handcuffed man was removed by the constables who had rushed in at the astonishing sound of shots in the peaceful office of the Assistant-Commissioner. He said: "Mr. Jellipot, I have a double reason for which to thank you. You have saved us from a most undignified possibility, and have also been opportune in supplying us with an unimpeachable reason for arresting a man of whose guilt I was less than sure."

Mr. Jellipot could not dispute the justice of the praise which he received. No man, however blameless on other grounds, can expect to retain his liberty if he discharges revolver shots in the office of an Assistant-Commissioner of the Metropolitan Police.

He said: "It seemed foolish to me, but I am afraid that the sudden sight of my young companions may have caused him to lose his head."

The remark directed attention upon those who had been reported to be in a very different and more perilous situation, and Mr. Jellipot went on to explain their presence.

"It appears," he said, "that there was a little misunderstanding—a very natural misunderstanding—concerning the extent of Miss Garten's previous acquaintance with the art of flying. She had, in fact, taken a course of instruction in Germany, at a time when aviation was very popular among the youth of that country, and before she commenced the associations which she has since, I feel sure, regretted.

"An incident in which she refused, for quite different reasons, to take the risks of the air, was interpreted in a way which led it to be supposed that she was as inexperienced in as she was averse from that somewhat hazardous method of transportation; and her subsequent denials, which do not appear to have been accompanied by the explanations she might have given, had there been a more real intimacy subsisting between herself and her late companions, seem to have been misapprehended and disbelieved.

"When the machine was very kindly left in her charge, she flew it back to the Croydon station, where she knew that a safe landing would be easy to find."

Sir William looked at her with the respect which those who have not yet joined in the conquest of upper air are inclined to feel for their more venturesome fellow-citizens. "It was," he said, "a very brave thing to do."

"There wasn't much in that," Miss Garten answered. "At least there wouldn't have been if they hadn't been so stingy in filling up. The real fright I got was when I thought Harold was going to kick against going, and I daren't give him any idea that they were setting us free in the way I had hoped they would."

Sir William said: "Well, I hope your troubles are over now." He spoke to Francis and Miss Garten equally, or so Mr. Jellipot took it to be. To the astute lawyer the opportunity was too good to miss. He reminded the Assistant-Commissioner that his client's appeal was still a fence to be overcome.

"Oh," Sir William said, in the good-humoured satisfaction he felt from the knowledge that the Rabone case was likely to end in a way that would redound to his own credit, and that of the efficient force it was his pleasure to rule, "I don't think he need trouble overmuch about that. There are ways—and ways—"

And Mr. Jellipot, for all his caution, was inclined to agree.

ABOUT THE AUTHOR

SYDNEY FOWLER WRIGHT (1874-1965) penned over seventy volumes of science fiction, fantasy, classic mysteries, historical novels, poetry, and non-fiction, many of them being published by the Borgo Press imprint of Wildside Press. Please visit his website at:

www.sfw.org

www.ingramcontent.com/pod-product-compliance
Lightning Source LLC
Chambersburg PA
CBHW021241260626
47155CB00004BA/1258